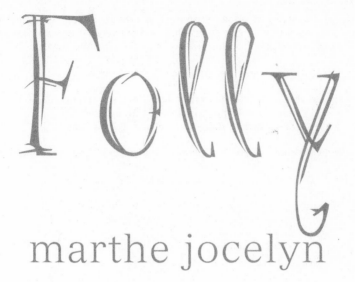

Folly

marthe jocelyn

WENDY
LAMB
BOOKS

Copyright © 2010 by Marthe Jocelyn

Wendy Lamb Books and the colophon are trademarks of Random House, Inc.

Visit us on the Web! www.randomhouse.com/teens

Educators and librarians, for a variety of teaching tools, visit us at www.randomhouse.com/teachers

Library of Congress Cataloging-in-Publication Data
Jocelyn, Marthe.
Folly / Marthe Jocelyn. — 1st ed.
p. cm.
Summary: In a parallel narrative set in late nineteenth-century England, teenaged country girl Mary Finn relates the unhappy conclusion to her experiences as a young servant in an aristocratic London household while, years later, young James Nelligan describes how he comes to leave his beloved foster family to live and be educated at London's famous Foundling Hospital.
ISBN 978-0-385-73846-0 (hardcover : alk. paper) — ISBN 978-0-385-90731-6 (lib. bdg. : alk. paper) — ISBN 978-0-375-89451-0 (e-book) — ISBN 978-0-375-85543-6 (pbk. : alk. paper) [1. Foundlings—Fiction. 2. Household employees—Fiction. 3. Foundling Hospital (London, England)— Fiction. 4. London (England)—History—19th century—Fiction. 5. Great Britain—History—Victoria, 1837–1901—Fiction.] I. Title.
PZ7.J579Fo 2010
[Fic]—dc22
2009023116

Printed in the United States of America
10 9 8 7 6 5 4 3 2 1

First Edition

FOR MY DAUGHTERS,
HANNAH AND NELL

MARY 1893

Telling

I began exceeding ignorant, apart from what a girl can learn through family mayhem, a dead mother, a grim step-mother, and a sorrowful parting from home. But none of that is useful when it comes to being a servant, is it? And nothing to ready me either, for the other surprises a girl might stumble over. Let no one doubt that I've learned my lesson and plenty more besides.

Imagine me back then, not knowing how silverware is to be laid out on a table, nor how to swill a stone floor or slice up the oddness of a pineapple; I did not know that tossing old tea leaves on the carpet works wonders toward collecting up the dust, nor how bluing keeps your white things white; I did not know how to write a letter and I had never had one come for me; I did not know what a man and a girl might do on a gravestone when they are crazy for each other; I did not know the heart were like a china teacup hanging in the cupboard from a single hook, that it could chip and crack and finally smash to the ground under a boot heel. And I did not know that even smithereens could reassemble into a heart. I did not know any of this.

This leads to that, Mam used to say. The trick is knowing where *this* begins and which *that* it might be leading to.

The kiss may not have been the start of things, but it led straight on to the rest of it, me without the slightest idea—well, maybe the slightest—of where it could end up. But one thing is certain: I were as ready for that first kiss as a girl can be. My hair were clean, my neck were washed, and my heart were banging away like a baby's fist on a pile of dirt.

That's jumping ahead of things, so I'll go back and tell what I do know—before and after the kiss, since we won't be hearing anything from Mr. Caden Tucker, will we?

Caden Tucker—scoundrel, braggart, and heart's delight. He'll never be seen again, not ever, so don't you waste your time. The officers claimed they couldn't find him and neither could I, for all I looked till my bosom would split with holding the ache. He'd have nothing to tell you that I can't, that I promise. He were cocky, but he weren't one to rely on for a true story, as it turned out.

I'll confess there were a part of me that shone bright in the sunshine cast by Caden Tucker as it never did elsewhere. A part of me that were *me,* the true Mary Finn, when I were walking out with him.

MARY 1876

Telling About Home in Pinchbeck, Lincolnshire

Our dad had his vegetables, grown for market or trade, or else he planted others' gardens. Winter times, when the ground were sleeping, he'd cut firewood or dig privies or whatever were asked for. Mam were kept busy with us, and the house, but we all helped, as a family does, you know. Though I suppose you're not familiar with the workings of a family.

We went each week to St. Bartholomew's, me taking the boys out to the graveyard when the sermon got them twitching.

"How many now?" I'd ask, and they'd tear up and down the rows, tapping the tops of each stone, shouting out the numbers, not thinking about Sunday or stomping on bones under the grass. But then it were Mam who changed the count and the game weren't so merry anymore.

Mam had four of us before birthing Nan, fifth and last. Mam died a week later, leaving me, just turned thirteen, to be mother as best I could. Until our dad went and found that Margaret Huckle a year after and put her in Mam's bed, thinking he were giving us a present somehow. Really it were like drowning nettles in the bottom of our tea mugs so every time we swallowed there were a sore patch, a blister, hurting deep inside in a way that couldn't be soothed.

That were the kind of talk that would have got me thrashed if anyone heard it, so it stayed quiet, right?

It were me, then Thomas, Davy, Small John, and the baby. Tall John Finn being our dad, meaning the one named for him could only be small.

Now, come Sundays, Dad said Thomas and Davy were big enough to stay plunked in the pew with him, so it'd be Small John and Nan in the churchyard with me. John were always coughing, not eager to run around. I devised other games for him. We picked out the letters on the stones, me knowing how to show him that much.

"Here's an *A*," he'd shout. "I found a *B*!" And after a while he made sense of the words.

"Crick!" he'd cry, or "*M* for Mason!" and I'd know he were right because Walter Crick were dead from pneumonia and Pauline Mason were the butcher's wife who died from a lump in her neck that stopped her swallowing.

Mam's stone were small next to some of the others, about the size of the church Bible, dawn-gray granite with pink flecks, traded for a year of potatoes.

Mary Ann Boothby Finn,

it said.

Wife of John
A Mother on Earth
An Angel in Heaven
b. 1843 d. 1876

Our dad, knowing Mam's favorites, planted bluebells and lily-of-the-valley. Come springtime they flourished so lush and pretty, even after that Margaret Huckle were thistling about at home, that I know he kept tending Mam's stone, though he never said.

I didn't go there often, not wanting to look sappy, talking to ghosts. I were leery too, of telling Mam only our miseries, so I'd wait till I had other news.

"Thomas lost another tooth," I'd say. "He looks a right fiend, pushing his tongue through the front, with his eyeballs crossed over. And Davy, he might be one of those Chinese monkeys that came with the fair, the way he jumps on chairs and swings about on gates. . . ."

Then I'd come to Small John and the worries would start. "He coughs, Mam, all night sometimes, though I make a warm garlic plaster like you showed me. I don't know if . . . well, I just don't."

My hands would go numb with me praying so hard she'd answer. I'd take a two-minute scolding if it meant she'd be there for two minutes. But the swallows would swoop, and the sun would sink, and the evening would sound hollow as an old bucket. The weight of things were on me alone. Along with our dad, of course.

I wonder now what you'd think of him, he not being like any man you've come across here.

I were little mother and he were keeping us fed and covered, strapping the boys when need be, but also telling stories at bedtime. During the day he were a grumbler, barely having enough words to finish out a sentence. But evenings, the boys would call, "Tell us one!" and in he'd come, and set at the end of the mat, with all of us tumbled together in the dark.

"It were a wild night," he'd start in a whisper meant to give us the shivers. "Rain so fierce it came down sideways. Lightning crackled like fire in a giant's grate, and thunder snapped. . . . There were such a blowing and a dashing of the rain, those poor travelers huddled like lost sheep beneath the lowest branches of an ancient evergreen. . . ." He'd let us picture the turbulent heavens, and the shadowy figures, and the damp needles scenting the air with earth and pine.

"Go on," we'd say. "Who were they?"

"Well," he might say. "It were the young Lord Thomas

Fortune and his servant Davy the Eager." Or, another time, "It were a boy named Bold Johnny with his magic puppy, Nana." Small John would push his best two fingers into his mouth with a happy smack, finally the hero.

Or, "It were the peasant lass, Mary, caught out in the storm, ever waiting for her father, lost while struggling home from a great battle against the Viking marauders. . . ."

Even if we'd had a nursery like I saw later in London for Master Sebastian, even if we'd had a whole bed each, we were used to each other's poky elbows and chill wee toes. We liked it best listening, and then sleeping, in a heap.

We'd have been content, going along like that, even without Mam. It were the arrival of that Margaret Huckle that were the next blow, like a tree through the roof.

I don't know how long our dad had known her or where they'd first met, sly-wise, but how I heard were like this:

"Mary." The boys were down at night and I were trying to mend Davy's shirt where the pig-nosed bully Ben Crick had torn it in a tussle at school.

"Yes, Dad." I bit off the thread.

"I've something to say will change things. Ease things for you."

I looked up, catching a whiff of peculiar.

"Since your mam died," he said, "you've been mother to the baby and Small John. And I thank you for it."

A shiver tickled the back of my neck, telling me *Watch out!* I'd never been thanked yet.

"But it's been more than a little girl should do," he said. "You've already got smudging under those bonny green eyes . . ." Him calling me *bonny*? Now my middle were apple jelly inside.

"I've found a woman who will be my wife."

"Your wife?" I repeated to be certain.

"She's a widow, losing her cottage near the Tumney farm where I go Thursdays." As if that explained. "She'll be a mother too," he said.

"But I'm doing it all just fine," I said. "It were hard when I were thirteen. But now I'm older. I'm better at it. I'll be fifteen next birthday. You don't have to fetch a new mother for us, not now." I could hear my voice go squeaking up. "We don't need a wife."

He patted my hand, lying there, holding the boy's shirt. "Her name is Margaret. Margaret Huckle. She's from over Spalding way. She's been a widow now for about a year. Her husband died, oh, March last, and she needs us as much as we need her."

"We don't need—"

"Think of Nan," he said.

"That's who . . . It's Nan, I'm . . . Nan's got *me*." I tapped my chest. "Me. Since she can't have Mam." But his finger went up, raised like an axe and swung to shush me.

I shook out Davy's shirt, tugged on the collar.

"She's going to live here?"

"I'll bring her for supper one day this week. She can see her new house and meet you all. We'll get ourselves married Sunday next, and have it done."

"Sunday next? But that's—" I stopped.

Our dad stood up. "It's your task to make her welcome. I'm off for my pipe." And out he went.

It were none of my business, I knew that. It were our dad, not us, who'd be sleeping next to her. But there were a lump in my belly like a week of cold porridge.

Wednesday came along and Dad said, "I've asked Dick Crebb for an old hen. If you'll make your cock-a-leekie, that'd be a fine way to show Margaret how we've been looking after things up until now. Tonight's the night."

Milk slopped over the lip of the pitcher while I poured into the boys' bowls.

"Spill," said Small John.

"Dress the chicken nice and make those potatoes with the crispy bits. She'll like those."

Small John's fingers stole to his mouth.

"Yes, Dad." I nodded while I were thinking up curse words.

So I went by Crebbs' after I'd walked the big boys to the schoolhouse, with Nan in my arms as always and Small John's fist dragging on my skirt. We collected the hen and I were relieved that Mrs. Crebb had plucked it.

"Maybe she'll be a jolly one," I whispered to Nan. "She doesn't have to be a disappointment. Maybe she'll know how to sew right, or make junket pudding that firms up proper. Maybe she'll sing, or say stories we haven't heard."

Maybe she'll be a mother, I thought, which only seems daft now. But not knowing yet, I could still wish. Maybe she'd help with the chores of having five children and there'd be a sliver of each day all my own.

Ha. Not ever did that happen until I were as alone as a soul can be and there's a lesson for you. Don't go wishing for what you know nothing about.

JAMES 1884

Home with the Peeveys

James was sick to be going. His whole six years of life he'd been waiting; they'd *all* been waiting, years. That was what happened to foster children. They had to go back when they stopped being little. But he didn't like it, not one bitty bit, however much they said it would be a new *adventure*. James didn't like adventures. Not then, and not later when he'd had a few.

"You'll be an explorer," they told him, but he knew that explorers met bugs and beasts and cannibals, so they couldn't trick James.

He didn't like new, he liked the same.

He liked the same he could keep account of.

ITEMS GOING WITH HIM:

- *1 shirt*
  (He did have a second shirt, but Mama Peevey thought it wouldn't be wanted, so it was left in Kent.)
- *1 pair of trousers*
- *1 pair of shoes*
- *A cap*
  (He'd be wearing all that, so did it count as being taken?)
- *A Bible (from the Reverend Kelly, that he'd never looked at, but he carried it along in case the Good Lord was watching. Maybe a Bible would show them at the Foundling that he was a good and honest boy, though he was pretty certain it was a sin to fib about being honest. He'd felt the strap from Mister P. often enough for what was called devilment, and he knew he fell short of being good, no matter what Mama Peevey said.)*
- *2 whistles, cut from willow by Mister's hand*
- *2 pencils from the shop and an account book, Mister knowing he liked to keep account of things*
- *2 peppermint sticks from the shop, his favorite. Mama Peevey slipped him a peppermint or a butterscotch on a rainy day. "Sugar is always sweet," she'd say. "But 'tis sweeter when the sky holds trouble." He remembered that.*

*CHILDREN OF JOAN PEEVEY AND
HER HUSBAND, MISTER FRANK PEEVEY:
Arthur Francis Peevey, who died as a baby
Himself, James Nelligan
Elizabeth Ellen Peevey, called Lizzy
Rose Frey*

Joan Peevey never claimed to be his mother. She was nursing Arthur and had milk to spare, so she took James on from the Foundling Hospital and nursed him too. Lucky thing, she always said, that the left-behind babies had women like Mama Peevey who could feed more than one. Then she bore Lizzy, her own, and fetched Rose, a foundling, because she'd shown the hospital she was good at fostering.

"The good Lord saw fit to take Arthur before he'd got his teeth, but that only left more room in my heart for you, didn't it, lovey?" she said to James. "When you try me like this, I tell the Lord you're being naughty enough for two boys. But really, you mean to be good, don't you, Jamie? Aren't you a good boy?"

This was after she'd cut off Rosie's hair because of him. He'd got boiled sweets from the shop and tucked them into Rosie's braids, to see if the colors would glimmer through like jewels. But they got stuck, right close to her scalp. Mama had tried with vinegar, but finally had to snip them out, Rose howling till her face went purple.

"Aren't you my good boy, James?"

Nodding didn't make it so.

"It's only hair!" he bellowed at Rose. "It'll grow again!"

He liked the shop best, where they played, and where he did his letters and his counting. It wasn't a real shop, like the butcher or Gibson's Bakery. There wasn't an awning, or a proper window. Mister Peevey put up shelves in the front room of the cottage, banging all up and down the walls, and shouting *Damn Jesus* when he banged himself. The coin box sat on a counter next to the stack of brown paper and twine for wrapping up packages.

Mister noticed early that James liked to count and to put the rows straight, so he set him a task each day, keeping records of the stock.

WHAT WAS IN THE SHOP:
- *Barrels of pickles and brown sugar and flour and rice*
- *Bottles of vinegar, bottles of bumpy relish, called "gentleman's," black sauce with too many letters called "wooster," red sauce called "piquant," and so many others, all different colors, Mister said to pour on flavor when the meat was boiled tasteless*
- *Matches, candles, lanterns that need dusting, but only by Mama P., her not trusting children with glass*
- *Rope, knives, hammers, and mallets—the villain's cupboard, James called it; no swords, but several boxes of poison for killing rats*
- *Ink, nibs, pencils, sealing wax, twine, and all what was needed for accounts or school or packages*
- *Sewing needles, spools of thread in every color, buttons, in sets of five or eight, stitched to painted cards that had gilt titles like: JUST THE THING! or LADIES' LOVELIES.*
- *Pins for sewing and pins for hair, nets and clasps and curved combs made from the shells of tortoises. James hated those combs, thinking of naked tortoises, until one day he sneaked them out and snapped each of them in two. He hid the pieces in the dirt next to the garden steps.*

- *Packets and packets of biscuits, oh, and the best thing! A whole row of huge glass jars, with lids too heavy for James to shift by himself.*

INSIDE THE JARS:
- *Peppermint sticks*
- *Toffees wrapped in gilt twists*
- *Sugar mice*
- *Licorice sticks, like rods of tar*
- *Boiled sweets, like lumps of ruby or emerald in a pirate's cache*

SOME FIRST WORDS
- *Peek Frean Ginger Crisps*
- *Hill, Evans & Co. Malt Vinegar*
- *Original and Genuine Lea & Perrins'*
- *Fry's Cocoa*
- *Epps's Cocoa*
- *Mooney's Biscuits*

Mama Peevey sat on the low stool by the door, just inside for rainy days, out on the step when the day was bright. James leaned against her knee for years, it seemed, with Toby Dog leaning on him, until Lizzy and then Rose took his place.

"Halloo there!" Mama would call to every passerby, and always get a call back. She'd chuckle, and pat a handkerchief against her neck, or her bosom, where he stared in wonder at the size of it. Nothing like his own skimpy chest, rib bones announcing themselves like so many tin soldiers.

James felt his insides wailing, preparing to leave the cottage and shop. She wasn't his born-from mother, but she was the only mother he'd ever known.

WHAT THE PEEVEYS HAD BEEN TELLING
JAMES ALL ALONG:
- *In London every building is as big as a church.*
- *In London James will eat meat every day.*
- *In London James will have a bed all to hisself.*
- *In London James will have new shoes every year and brass buttons on his jacket.*
- *In London there is a queen. (Lizzy wanted more than anything to meet Queen Victoria and be adopted as a princess, so it was her who added that bit.)*

They'd had a hundred goodbyes and boohoos all week—at breakfast, dinner, suppertime, prayer time, and every minute in between. One or the other of them would be leaking about how it was the last bun he'd be eating out of that oven or the last taste of potato soup sprinkled with chives from Mama's garden or the last time there'd be a boy in the house, how it'd be them still together and him far away . . . one mournful reminder after the next until he put fingers into his ears and held his breath, hoping his eyeballs would pop out.

Finally, Mama Peevey said he'd done his last chore. He was to take Toby Dog outside and say goodbye to Martin. James was more than six but his friend Martin was nearly eight, so he was bigger. He lived over the road with two brothers even bigger than him. He had a real mother, and a stepfather named Bart who Martin called Fart but only with his brothers and James. Having all those biggers around, Martin thought he knew everything.

Lizzy had been stuck on James like a shadow all day, so she was following close when Martin said, "Hey, last chance to hit the cabbages." They stood side by side at the edge of the porch to see who could pee furthest into the garden, and it was Martin, like always, being bigger.

"That's nasty," said Lizzy.

She wouldn't let Rose come outside to look. There was a struggle with the door and fingers got pinched and more whimpering and what Mister called bellyaching. Martin and James sneaked off and sat on crates next to the shed, whistling some, but quiet after a bit, watching evening coming. The sky was smudged with pink between the gray clouds.

"Last night I listened," said Martin. "When I was in bed. My mother said something maybe you want to know."

"You shouldn't listen to her," James told him. "Your mother is an old gossip, my mother says."

"She's not your mother."

"I know that."

"She had another boy."

"I know that. Is that your secret? I know all about Arthur. He died when we were babies. Turned blue, he did."

"There's a part you don't know." Martin picked up a stick.

"What?"

"When Arthur died, Mrs. Peevey was brokenhearted, my mother said. Cracked right in two, my mother said. She was going to pretend to the London hospital that it was you who died."

"What?" said James. "What do you mean?"

"She wanted to tell them it was the orphan baby who died. So she could keep you. She was that miserable, losing Arthur. She just wanted to have you for always, and to tell them a lie."

James's head was wobbly as if he'd been smacked with Mister's big hand. He sat very still, taking in a long breath in case a sob burped out.

"So, you know why she didn't?" Martin was digging with the end of his stick, spraying dirt over their toes.

"Stop that," James told him, shaking his foot. "Why didn't she?"

"Mister Peevey said no. He said the money was needed."

"The money?"

"They get money for you. Don't you know anything? They get allowance, my mother calls it. To pay for what you eat and your clothes." He poked the stick into another hole, grinding it in.

James looked down at his trousers, patched with Mama Peevey's tidy stitches. "But now I'm going anyhow," he said. "Tomorrow."

"That's right," said Martin. "Now they lose you *and* the money. But this way, at least, they had al*low*ance till you were six."

"But . . ." James rubbed a new worn spot above his knee. "The other way they could have kept me forever, saying I was Arthur."

"Your dad wanted the money."

"He's not my dad."

"Yeah, my mother says Lord knows who your dad might be, but at least he must have been a handsome blighter. She was blabbing all this to my auntie Molly last night when I was in my bed. But then they talked about baking raisin bread, so I went to sleep."

In the morning, James tried to chew a hunk of bread while Mama Peevey dressed him as if it were Sunday. Around his neck she hung the cord with a band dangling from it, his number pressed deep into the tin: 847229. Rose had one too, but she wouldn't be needing it for nearly four years.

Mama Peevey looked at James and tilted her head and clucked her tongue. "Ah, the curls on you," she said. "You should have been a girl. With those eyelashes? You'll be a heartbreaker, mark my words."

He didn't think being a girl was anything to wish for and a heartbreaker didn't sound so excellent either, so he wasn't surprised when Mister stuck his nose in.

"What does he want to be a pretty boy for? He'll be better off knowing how to fight."

"He's only six!" she said.

"More than six," said James.

"Six?" said Mister. "And never had a bloody nose?"

"Don't you dare!" said Mama Peevey, jumping up in a hurry. And Mister laughed, pretending to land his fist on James.

"Never had a black eye? That'll change at the big school in London, you mark my words. You pick your friends with care up there," said Mister. "You'll want to be giving black eyes, not getting them." And out he went to watch for the cart.

"Make me a nice cup of tea, will you, Jamie?" said Mama Peevey. "It'll be the last I get till the girls are growed two or three years."

They sat on the bench by the table, waiting for the kettle to boil, her stroking James's hair with her fingers, counting the minutes of his very last hour.

"I want to stay with you," he told her.

"I've got nothing pretty to say," she whispered. "No way to fix things." Tears rolled across her freckled cheeks. James hid his face in her lap so he couldn't see. He couldn't ask her, either, about what Martin had said.

Then Rose woke up, just what they hadn't wanted, and started her bleary-eyed mewling. Mister scooped her up, pressing her mouth to his shoulder. He pushed Mama and James out into the street where the cart was waiting, sent from the Foundling to bring them in. James winged a pebble toward Martin's window but it didn't get there, just fell with a *thip* in the dust.

They were three to start: the driver, Mama Peevey, and James. They picked up more foundlings along the way, but it was only them at dawn, peering back from the joggling seat, waving goodbye to Rose and Mister till they blurred with the road.

MARY 1876

Telling About That Margaret Huckle

My mam and our dad knew each other all their lives in the village, meaning from being children up till sixteen when they began to walk out and, I'll guess, lie down as well. They were married two years and lost a baby and then had me when Mam was twenty years old.

I didn't think about love, not till later, not till I were so blighted myself. I suppose my parents loved each other as much as they'd time for, with a swarm of children and Dad's vegetables and Mam's scrubbing and sewing, and all of it crowded into our little house. There weren't the spats or blistering words as I've heard elsewhere. We'd got too much work for such bother.

But that were long ago. Now we had Her.

"Her face is bumpy," said Davy. "Like she's saving currants in her cheeks for later."

"Her nose too," said Thomas. "More bumps than nose."

"Yellow," said Small John.

"I wish she were pretty," said Davy.

Pretty? Call a rotting potato prettier. Call a turnip with fungus on it prettier.

Not safe to say out loud, true facts like that. Little boys take words and carry them like so many treats, to sprinkle on other ears. That were the lesson I learned in our crowded cottage and in our lane brimming with chatterboxes: Never say anything you don't want said again.

That Margaret Huckle liked us mum. She hadn't any babies of her own, remember, she didn't know yet how a supper table could be, bursting with questions and spillage and jokes and fussing. She expected the grace, For-what-we-are-about-to-receive-may-the-Lord-make-us-truly-thankful-Amen, and then quiet, perhaps the clink of a knife or steady obedient chewing until the next grace, Thank-you-for-these-blessings-we-remain-in-service-O-Lord.

"Are you not going to send these hollering imps to the wall? John Finn, are you not? Then I shall!" And up she'd get, porridge stick in hand, ready to raise welts.

"Ah, now, Maggie dear," our dad would say on a good day, putting a hand on her arm, patting-like. "They're a bit rowdy, I see that, but they're children. Let's finish here and I'll take them to task later."

That were if his knees weren't aching or his back weren't pinching or his hands weren't raw from digging. On those days he'd be so weary that he didn't notice the uproar all around him and just sat with his jaw grinding away at whatever it met until Margaret Huckle began her tirade.

"Are you that deaf, John Finn, that you don't hear the devils howling at your own table? Are you deaf on top of dirty?"

He'd raise his face, surprised, it seemed, to find us there. He'd tug on his sleeves, knowing what offended, trying to cover his knuckles, as gray and grubby as roots, as knotted and gnarled. Up he'd look, suddenly hearing our noise. He'd see the furrows in his wife's potato face and he'd snarl, *"Shut it!"*

My brothers would shut it in an instant, wiggling their bottoms back to sitting on the bench, Small John catching his breath with a whimper. Only Nan would set off wailing, scared by the bark, and that were my chance to catch her up and leave the cottage with a shawl around us both, as if bringing peace to Margaret Huckle's evening were my greatest wish.

We'd go walking, Nan and me, and I'd sing "Twinkle, Twinkle, Little Star" while we looked up at the sky strewn with silvery dots. I'd look up, anyway. Nan only cared to look at me and tap her teeny fingers at my chin or blink or sometimes chuckle, out there with the swirling night breeze in the lane.

We'd go back in eventually, and I'd tuck Nan into her cradle that were half an ale keg, really, that our dad put rockers on. He'd made it for Thomas but it still were sturdy; only been repaired once, after they'd piled in together for a pirate ship tossing on a stormy sea.

I'd wash the boys' faces and make them do their own hands. I'd daub the worst dirt off the hems of things. I'd hear their prayers and polish their little white nubs of teeth with a soft cloth, Margaret Huckle not knowing to do any of it, and her new husband, John Finn, depending on me since Mam.

The boys were good at night, unless Small John peed the mat, but even then the others'd just sleep while I peeled off his wet shirt and laid down dry flannel or papers as best I could.

"They're like unbroken animals," Margaret Huckle said, gleamy wee eyes like beetles in a tub of bread dough. "Never trained right, and what chance do I have this late in the game? If they'd been mine . . . well . . . there'd be plenty different. . . ."

When I heard her slandering Mam and me, it made my teeth sharpen up like a hedge clipper.

"They only misbehave when they're mistreated," I said. "They're boys."

"Filthy boys."

"Getting muddy is like eating supper, just a part of the day." *And what difference does it make to you? As I'm the one doing the washing?*

I had no practical idea for how to change our lot, except for wishing it would change. My wishes were about Her breaking a leg and suffering unspeakable pain before the infection set in, so her limb got swelled and festering before it were chopped off with rusty shears. And then she'd die, of course, and not a one of us missing her, not even our dad.

I never once imagined it would be me leaving instead, me being forced to abandon the little ones to go some-where so lonely and dismal that I'd be sick, aching for home, and find myself wondering if that Margaret Huckle were really so ugly? Or were I making up stories?

JAMES 1884

Arriving Back

The Foundling Hospital looked like a mighty fortress. All the stories about London houses were true, it seemed, seeing those brick walls climb up toward the sky at the end of a driveway so long you'd expect Queen Victoria herself at the end of it. Mama Peevey squeezed James's hand as the cart trundled its rickety way through the gates.

"We're like mice," he said. "And that's the dragon's cavern."

"Brave mice," she said, but her eyes were drippy and neither of them was brave. There was a man in a tight black coat at the top of the stairs, peering down.

"A male charge?" His voice came out like dull taps. "Leave him in the room to the left, madam. You proceed to the offices on the right, where you will complete a report in accordance with the regulations. . . ."

Mama Peevey nudged James through the door on the left and stepped away. Suddenly he could scarcely see or hear for the hot sting in his eyes and the drumming in his ears. He was in a place wider and taller than he'd ever seen indoors. A line of boys, most of them five or six like him, stood fidgeting, with several more sitting on a bench by the wall. Every one of them was wearing a nightshirt over drawers.

An older boy swooped over, as big as Martin's brother Wes. Unlike the small boys, he was wearing a funny brown suit with a red waistcoat. James didn't dare look at him, really, except to see his chin was dotted with pimples, also like Wes.

"They come off," he said, pointing.

The big boy meant his clothes. There, in front of everyone. Mister had said his second shirt wouldn't be needed, but James had not considered what that meant.

He couldn't feel his own fingers groping to lift his shirt. His heart clamored like the wheels of an ice cart. *Bare-naked mouse,* he thought. *Without even fur.* James was all the way naked, *naked,* before the big boy finally handed over a nightshirt and pants and snatched the bundle of old clothes.

"And don't go pissing the bed," he said. "This is all you'll have till we've got a suit to fit." He carried James's belongings out into the hallway, while James scrambled into the new ones, ducking his hot face low as he could. What if he did piss the bed? What did that boy go saying things like that for? What horrible thing would happen next?

There was a man wearing a shirt with no waistcoat or jacket, showing big blurs of sweat under his arms, huffing a little with every breath. He'd have been grim enough, just standing there, but he was holding a pair of scissors twice the size of Mama Peevey's sewing shears, and he was wielding the blades upon the heads of one boy after another, set on a stool in front of him.

"I want my da!" someone cried, and that started a chorus all over the room.

"Mama!"

"Take me home!"

"I want my da!"

James was fixed upon those scissors. They trembled with every piercing whine. The barber's feet shuffled in the grass of mingled hair: russet, golden, chestnut, jet.

Did the Peeveys know about this? Did they know the truth about what was waiting for him? Did they knowingly tell him those lies, or were they tricked too?

His heart stopped its wild race and lay as sharp and heavy as a brick in his chest. None of that crying, none of those stranger boys could change anything, none of it would change the lie he'd been told about the glories of London.

It came to be James's turn on the stool. The man's stink swished the air as he snipped. James squeezed his eyes shut, not daring to plug his nose. The room full of whimperings faded behind the man's phlegmy little grunts. James's fingernails dug through the nightshirt into his legs so he wouldn't scream.

"Done." The barber sent him, bald and patchy, to join the others on the bench.

The boy next to James was jiggling like his sister Lizzy outside the privy, making the whole row jiggle along with him. James reached over to touch his knee. He stopped for a moment, darting James a wild look, before starting up again. The next boy came from the scissor man and plopped down. His face was sun-freckled but his scalp was white through the stubble.

A fuss at the door, and the fostering mothers were herded in across the grand room for a final look. Was it half an hour since Mama Peevey had left him here? Only minutes more at most. The mothers had made their reports and were going outside into the sensible world. They would climb back into rickety carts, sit on splintered seats with cursing drivers, and journey home alone.

Mama Peevey held James's shirt, his patched trousers, his stockings. Her gaze wavered back and forth, scanning the crowd of identical boys in white nightshirts. They'd sprung up, calling out "Mama," every one of them. James was waving madly, but so were all of them. She glanced his way but she was weeping and didn't pause, not knowing him without his dark curls. As she was led out, she pressed the wool of his shirt against her whole face, as if it were still on his back, as if she were giving him one last sniff.

MARY 1877

Telling About the Rogue and Scholar

"It's a good chance for you, Mary," said our dad, for the twentieth time. "Margaret thinks—"

I couldn't listen again to what measly thinks Margaret were having.

"I'll go," I said. It were unavoidable. "Only to be earning some of my own money, so I'm not taking from the littles. You'll see how much I'm missed. I'm not agreeing to please anyone, especially her."

"We're giving you a chance, Mary. To . . . venture out, you know . . ."

It were Her plot to be rid of me, sending me to work for her sister, under pretense of *opportunity*. Ha.

"You'll be here through Christmas, of course," said Dad. "And go off in the new year. New year, new paths to tread on, eh?"

As it turned out, this leads to that, for better or worse.

Christmas were a gloomy one, though I didn't let on to my brothers. We made paper garlands, like always, and strung them up, till She said they were like to catch fire. We swallowed her goose, dry as old bones, and shared out the oranges.

I went off only a few days after, wearing a dress cut down by that Margaret Huckle. It'd been hers, for Sundays, but she took inches off the bottom and tucked in the sides, humming all the while, so tickled she were to be seeing the last of me. That, and her own new baby coming. As if that were anything special, were what I thought at fourteen. It'd make you sick if I told you about the row of crying brothers my last morning. But the picture that's stuck in my head is of Margaret Huckle holding on to Nan, who were bawling like she'd just been birthed in a snowstorm. Months later I'd bang my head trying not to picture it, but it's there still. My dad drove me over in the cart, more than half the day to get there. That farewell were not pretty.

One gent on the painted sign had a wily tilt to his eyebrows, with his hand in the pocket of the other gent, who carried a book under his arm. This were the Rogue and Scholar, public house and inn; thirty-nine miles and as far from our cottage in Pinchbeck as the man in the moon.

The lettering on the sign were writ in gold, making a fancy impression that were not upheld within. My first step into the barroom, I near swooned at the stink of beer

and spirits, of pipes and spat-out tobacco. Stools and tables were crammed in tight together under a low ceiling,
making me wish hard for a meadow so I could take one
breath that weren't poison.

They had four rooms upstairs to let, though only one
or two were occupied most nights, the place being a little off the main road. It were mainly where the men of the
village stopped by most evenings for a smoke, a pint of
ale, and a bit of boasting or remorse. Margaret Huckle's
dead husband had spent his waking hours and many
coins in the very room where I now found myself each
morning, yanking at the windows and propping open the
door, begging a chill breeze to freshen air so thick you
could chew it.

If Margaret Huckle looked like a potato, her sister,
Fanny Forbes, had more of the rice pudding about her
features: soft and speckled and bland. Billowy soft in the
flesh, but rough and cranky in her disposition. The reason
for her cloudy outlook were clear to all, and that reason
were named Mr. Forbes. If he weren't belching, he were
passing gas. If he weren't making fumes, he were touching his own self, and if he weren't fiddling under his apron
while all the world watched, he were waiting to rub his
sausagey fingers across someone else's backside.

I were at the Rogue and Scholar only sixty-seven days
but it were enough to cry lakes full, missing my kidlings,
enough to learn a new set of curse words I'd never heard
till then, along with plenty of reasons to use them.

Enough so that I snatched the chance to escape when it appeared—in the fine, manly shape of Harry Bates. Not that I considered romance, him being old, near thirty years.

But if it weren't for Bates, sitting at the table in the kitchen at the Rogue and Scholar, with his boots off and his feet hooked up on a chair while he ate a bowl of Fat Pat's beef stew, well . . . it'd be like a bedtime story, imagining what *might* have happened elsewise.

He winked at me while I filled his cup, me nearly pouring into his lap and him grinning like an alligator. I set about mopping up the splashes and he winked again, liking the disturbance.

"Mary!" Fat Pat just about walloped me with her voice alone. I jumped and teetered on my own feet, face as hot as a griddle while Bates laughed out loud, smacking his palm on the table.

"You, sir," said Fat Pat, threatening him with her spoon. "You leave the girl to do her work. Do you see she's half your age? And she's not much at the best of times, on her last warning with the missus."

"I was only hoping," he said, "as I'd find a clever girl in the house who could look in on my mistress up there in one of those rooms."

There were nothing so far to indicate that I might have a single clever bone in my body, so I knew from the start he were the flattering type.

"She's up there with a sickly baby," he went on.

"Mrs.—though not for long, I'll warrant—*Mrs.* Overly. Could you slip up there? Tell her Bates sent you."

I looked to Fat Pat and got a sigh and a nod. Mrs. Overly were in the so-called Victoria Room, it being the best and no one else looking for a bed at midday.

The baby's cries met me on the stairs. I tapped on the door but weren't surprised with no answer, the air being filled with caterwauling. I poked my head around the door, knowing it were rude, but better than hammering with my boot, which were what I'd need to do to be heard.

There sat the lady with her hands over her ears and tears pouring out of her eyes while the baby lay on the bed kicking like an upturned june bug, its face scrunched and red as an old berry. The noise—Lordy!—were enough to make your head split open. The lady, Mrs. Overly, jumped up and grabbed on me, pulling me to the bed.

"He's dying," she cried. "There is something terribly wrong!" She touched him with a dainty white finger and pulled back as his howling went up another note.

I gathered his fierce little body into my arms, while his fists and legs did battle. I wrapped the blanket tight to hold him still and pressed my humming lips to his throbbing temple, rubbing his back in firm circles.

I were tossed straight back to those nights with Nan, remembering how minutes would pass while I prayed for the shudder of peace. It took only a moment with this little one. He burped a burp so huge that the mother squeaked and flung her fingers to her mouth, as if I'd forced out a demon. Then all were quiet, till he gurgled and tipped his face to look at me.

The mother's eyes were like candles in a cellar, beams of joy, despite the puffiness. "However did you do that? What was wrong with him?"

"It were only wind!" I said. "Do you not have a nurse-maid?"

"We had one, but now . . . We only need to get to London," she said. "Mama is hiring a new one for me. . . ." She touched her baby's face, but did not try to take him back.

"I . . . I shouldn't really tell a servant," she said. "But . . . I've been . . . I've been . . . I was . . . *married!*" Her voice cracked and tears came sniveling out all over again. "But I don't think I am anymore! Everything has turned . . . dreadful."

She covered her eyes with her hands, crying away. I bounced the baby, who were now quite merry. Should I pat his mother too? I waited, and waggled him, and shortly she wiped her eyes.

"I'll be *fine*," she said, as if reminding herself. "I'll take the baby now."

When I tried to hand him over, he protested with a jerk and a sharp cry. The mother sank to the bed and wept in earnest.

Lordy, I thought. *Mrs. Forbes'll have my hide.*

"I . . . I . . . I've never been alone with the baby yet!" she wailed. "Nurse Polley was with us from when he was born. She took care of things, until she left. . . . It was such a scene you wouldn't believe! She said terrible things about . . . well, that my husband . . . oh, I shouldn't be telling you this!"

No, you most certainly shouldn't.

"She called me . . . a *ninny*!" She gulped. "She said that Harold was . . . a lass . . . lascivious cur, whatever that is, and that she wouldn't stay another minute. . . ." She gripped the edge of the bed, stopping the shakes for a moment.

"I . . . don't know what to do," she whispered. She looked up and remembered that I was holding her son. I offered him again, and again he clung to me.

"Oh, couldn't you just keep him?"

"I've got work, miss. Mrs. Forbes will be wondering."

"But I can't bear it if he cries again. I really can't. I shall run screaming from the room."

I believed her. But it weren't my business. A hundred tasks awaited me, with not one of them being to cuddle a miserable baby whose mother didn't know which end were leaking.

"He needs a change." My hand were now holding damp flannel.

Her eyes puzzled up and then widened. "Oh! Oh, dear! I don't . . ." She looked vaguely about the room, spying her case, and faltering at once.

"A change?"

I were too familiar, I know, but my arms were tired

from holding her child, cursed with a foolish mother. I laid him on the bed beside her, no matter that he puckered up and squawked.

"Miss, if you don't mind me saying, the baby has certain needs that you'll have to attend to. A clean, dry bottom is one of them."

"Oh, please!" She looked desperate. "Oh, please, I beg you! What is your name?" She fell to her knees and held on to my wrists as if I'd fly away, which I sorely wished I'd been capable of doing.

"Mary."

"Mary, dear Mary. Won't you please help me? I will pay you, I promise, more than your wages here. Find me a cloth for him and I'll give you . . ." She looked about the room again and then to her own clothing. "I'll give you this lace handkerchief . . . and five shillings and—"

"Miss, I don't think—"

"My name is Lucilla," she said. "Lucilla Overly. My father is Lord Sherman Allyn, the historian. You've heard of him?"

I had not, of course.

"And this baby is sure to die if you don't help me. We are supposed to be moving on from here in an hour or so, after the horses are fed and"—she barked a laugh that were not a pretty sound—". . . and the baby has *rested* with me, that's what Bates said. That I should lie down to sleep!"

"Perhaps you should do that, miss." The baby's cries

were gathering strength, so my suggestion were ridiculous and we both knew it. I picked him up, I couldn't not. As if I could leave Nan wailing or anyone else.

I tucked him into the bodice of my apron.

"May I use a stocking, miss?"

She rummaged in the case and found one. She watched while I strapped the baby more securely to my chest.

"I'll take him for one hour, miss, and you have your little lie-down. But he'll soon need feeding, too, won't he?"

She winced. "The wet nurse . . . I didn't think . . . I've stopped my own milk weeks ago."

I spun around and marched out the door. She were a certain danger to her own child.

In the hallway I could hear Mrs. Forbes calling up the back stairs, "Mary? Wherever is that lazy girl? *Mary?*"

ELIZA 1877

Telling About Mary

Bates come in, smirking at Cook and Eliza. "You're looking at the hero of the day," he said, plucking up an apple from the bowl on the table and rubbing it to a shine on his sleeve.

"What's got you so pleased with yourself?" asked Mrs. Wiggins. "Did you collect poor Miss Lucilla from that husband we all knew was a brute?"

"I did. As well as her wretched baby, whose squawking never stopped from the front door in Waterford to the shack of a country inn where I performed my heroic act." His teeth bit into the apple with such a crunch Eliza could taste the juice herself.

"And what was that?" she asked. "Did you drown the brat?"

"Eliza, you hush!" Mrs. Wiggins always scolded for disrespect, but it made Bates laugh so Eliza could not resist.

But this time, "No," with that smirk again. "I found a lass." If his mustache had been long enough, he'd have been twirling it. " 'Hello?' I says to myself," said Bates. " 'What we've got here is a damsel in distress. . . .' Two damsels, really, with Miss L. on the one side and this baby-taming wench on the other. There's nothing like a damsel to turn a man into a hero, is there? So I brought her fine green eyes along to Neville Street."

Eliza swore she could almost see his trousers take shape in the front. But then he caught her eyes looking down there and he smirked extra, making a little thrust with his hips in a way Mrs. Wiggins wouldn't see. Eliza quick turned her face to peeling the apples and vowed to hate this girl, whoever she might be. Bates was a brute the way he played with her, but oh, what he could do with his hands in a dark place!

She wouldn't be the one to tell him all his fancy dancing was for naught.

"You're a little behind the news, Mr. Bates," said Mrs. Wiggins. "There's already a nursemaid in residence."

"And a sour cow she is too," muttered Eliza.

"Eliza Pigeon, you watch your sass."

"Oh no," said Bates. He dropped his apple core into the bin. "Who's she, then?"

"Her name," said Mrs. Wiggins, "is Miss Hollow. Miss Judith Hollow."

Bates sat down and shot his eyes toward the ceiling, as if he could see straight through and up to where this *lass* of his was likely being tossed out the door.

Eliza's intention to despise Mary Finn was flummoxed when she finally come downstairs. Eliza saw a skimpy young thing, so fresh from the country you could smell the dung and the blossoms right off her. Carroty hair and eyes more the color of old parsley than real green. No tits to speak of, nothing for Bates to ogle, Eliza assured herself of that straightaway. Knowing how he liked an ample handful, she softened up considerable. She could do with the help, after all. She could put the new girl on laundry and save herself a parcel of neck pain. Oh, and potatoes, and donkeying, and water-lugging; all the meanest tasks were suddenly half the weight of yesterday.

So Eliza let herself be fooled in the beginning, she'd admit that. Mary had one of those faces they called *heart-shaped* in the penny novels, meaning to tell you *adorable* and *prettier-than-the-reader-could-ever-hope-to-be*. She tricked you just by tilting her showy-haired head, that she was a sweet girl. Well, Eliza soon learned, didn't she? The girl who plays the angel in the Christmas pageant might be making her only visit to church all year. Otherwise occupied, unless Eliza were mistaken.

So, this Mary Finn come down, looking like she'd been served porridge when she'd expected roast beef.

"Sit yourself down," said Cook. "You can peel apples while you tell us how you've come to be here."

That was Cook testing Mary's skill with a knife, and she showed herself well enough able. And out pours the story: how she'd helped the baby stop crying, how it was only wind, how Miss Lucilla—who she called Mrs. Overly—had begged her to come to London with a promise of an upstairs situation, how Bates had been so kind, how Lady Allyn took one look at her and—no wonder!—declared her unfit as a nursemaid, how Miss Lucilla blushed and pouted, how Mary felt what she called "drumming terror" that she'd be sent out into what she called "those London streets," how Lady Allyn had relented and allowed that Mary could work in the scullery on trial, and how Mrs. Wiggins was to be judge of what Mary called "any hope for a future" . . .

"And where'll she be sleeping?" asked Eliza, as if Mary weren't sitting there with the face of doom.

"With you, dear," said Cook, who only used *dear* once a month when she had a need for something.

Mary arrived with her dress and her stockings, though they were worn enough they might have been made of cheesecloth. She had on a pair of boots she said used to be her dad's. Later, she traded them with the boy, Nut, from the workhouse, whose feet were near big enough to fit. The shoes he'd got were chapped like old skin but the right size for Mary. That was how they got to be friends—no one else would talk to him, the little beast, but Mary would, having brothers and knowing little boys. According to Mary, they weren't always thinking about toads or farts, but sometimes about their mothers—not that Nut had one of those—or battles or a fistful of sugar from the breakfast bowl. Mary was good at pinching sugar and letting Nut lick her thumb. As if he were a baby, scoffed Eliza. He must be fully nine or ten, just smaller in mind.

Eliza wasn't too pleased to have Mary sleeping in her bed when she'd had it to herself for the three months since Hazel was so foolish as to get caught in the study filling a flask with gin at Christmas. She'd been a hard one, that Hazel. Eliza wasn't saying Mary was anything like Hazel. Her method was not so plain to see. But one thing *was* clear: Mary was new to service, and if it hadn't been for Eliza, she'd have been lost. She did learn quick, but every time she watched Eliza first.

"Have you even read the book, Mary?" asked Eliza, the second night they were tiptoeing around each other before climbing under the blanket.

"The book?" And she looked scared, so Eliza knew she couldn't read, along with her other useless qualities.

"Aye, the book. *Baylis Handbook, Law of Domestic Servants.*"

"No," said Mary. "No, I've not had the pleasure."

Ha.

Next morning, she was stumbling over the order of things when Bates come along and said, "If you're not catching on quick enough, Mary, just give His Lordship a glimpse of your . . . attributes . . . and you won't get a scolding."

Eliza was thinking, *What attributes? There's barely enough there to fill a chemise!* But, "Don't pay no mind to Bates," she told Mary. "He's a cheeky, but he means no harm."

"I've met worse," Mary said. "He was nice enough to get me here."

"Not too nice, I hope," said Eliza. "I fancy him myself, so keep clear, if you don't mind."

That was when Mary flashed such a bright, warm smile Eliza knew later what made the men go soft on her.

"Oh, nothing to worry about there!" laughed Mary. "He's a bit old for me, wouldn't you say?"

She was cheerful, Eliza could see that, and it was a relief to share the load, after doing it herself for all those weeks since Hazel.

"I wonder could you help me out?" Mary asked. "I've a note to write home and . . . my letters are not so well formed as they might be."

So Eliza wrote down what Mary told her, about leaving the other position and coming to the Allyns of Neville Street for an *opportunity*. Eliza wasn't sure of the spelling, but Mary insisted she use that word. Eliza could see that the story was longer than the few lines written, but it didn't seem right to poke about just yet.

Many was the time later that Eliza thought Mary might have been her friend, if only she'd left Bates alone.

OLIVER 1884

All Foundlings Being the Same

Oliver Chester knew that the anguish of adjustment was the same for every boy coming in from fostering; each faced a suffering he'd never imagined. Some were embarrassed, some toughed it out, some took longer than others to recover, depending on what sort of family they'd come in from. But Oliver remembered those nights in the dark and those queues to wash and eat. He saw their little noses twitching with the effort not to cry and he felt weak all over again. Never enough food, cold rough sheets, unexplained routines, and the towering Big Chaps who seemed as though they might very well murder you. It had been just the same in his time.

That was why he preferred to wait, actually. He liked to teach the older ones, once they'd left what was called the

Infant School. By the time they got to be Big Chaps—all of eight or nine years old—they were broken in and no longer spilling sadness at odd moments, though there were still one or two each year who managed to crack his heart.

But as long as he prepared his lessons and delivered his lectures and meted out work for revision, he escaped knowing most of the boys. They wore uniforms, after all; it was best that they *be* uniform as well. He managed to prevent them from having any curiosity about him, or the outside world.

It was the challenge of his life, actually, to evade curiosity, though it pestered him when he least expected to have his thoughts interrupted. It was an irony, Oliver Chester realized, that a history master should avoid his own history, but after all, wasn't that what he'd been taught to do from the start?

JAMES 1884

What the Chaplain Told Them

There were fourteen new boys brought in that Sunday evening, though James was surprised when he counted; it seeming like more than that. After the haircut, each boy was given a scrubbing. At the Peeveys' they'd had their baths in the barrel every week, or in the stream during the summer. Each night before supper they'd got what Mama P. called *licked behind the ears,* using a wet cloth.

This scrubbing at the Foundling was like being given a new skin, only the old one needed to come off first. The soap was gritty and smelled horrible. The brush felt as though it were made from thorns. The boys yelped, raw and shivering. James had managed not to cry again since Mama went away through that door, but he was very nearly leaking tears by the end of the bath.

There was supper of bread and hard white cheese, and afterward they were taken into a room with softly gleaming wooden walls and a carpet on the floor like thick blue moss. The children sat on two benches, rigidly listening to a man with a puffy face and bristling side whiskers. While he spoke to them, he frequently tapped his own left cheek, as if he were pointing to himself. James began to count.

"Good evening, boys." *One.*

A mumbled response from only a few prompted the man to repeat, "My name is Mr. Byrd. Good evening, boys." *Two.*

"Good evening, Mr. Byrd."

"Ah, much better." *Three.* Was he touching a sore spot, James wondered. "I am the chaplain of the Foundling Hospital and will be your counselor on many matters for many years to come. Although you are no doubt weary this evening"—*four*—"it is important that you go to your prayers and to your new beds with certain thoughts in mind." *Five.* James glanced at the boy next to him, wishing it were Martin, so their elbows could bump to share the oddness of this man's finger. Martin would cross his eyes and pretend to choke—

"Each of you is known to us as a child of shame."

What? Six.

"Your. Mothers. Are. Sinners. It is vital that you never forget that you are the progeny of sin. It is therefore your duty to devote yourselves to goodness and servitude. Thanks to the generosity of the governors of this great institution, you have been rescued from the certain peril of becoming sinners yourselves. In your prayers tonight, and on all other nights, you are hereby appointed—"

James giggled. Ap*point*ed! While he was *pointing*! *Seven. Eight.* A glare from Mr. Byrd.

"—to thank God for your salvation, and to offer humble obedience and gratitude from this day forward for as long as you shall live." *Nine.*

Mr. Byrd fell silent and for a moment was still. James shifted, sliding his hands under the coarse white fabric that covered his knees. What was the man talking about? The way the words rolled out made it sound important, but James—*ten*—had been counting the finger-tapping-the-cheek and had not listened properly. Was he now supposed to be doing something? The man moved his stare from one boy to the next, as if—*eleven*—he were examining them. James held his breath. His turn.

"You—"

James jumped, but realized the man was only starting up again. He did not mean "you, James," he meant "you, all you boys." This was *hard*! Why had Mama brought him here?

"You carry names given to you through the generosity of the hospital governors. You will be fed and clothed and taught through the charity of the hospital governors." *Twelve.* "You will not spend a single hour of your life occupied in idleness, dishonesty, or ingratitude. Will you, boys?" *Thirteen.*

"No, Mr. Byrd."

"You will instead be industrious, honest, and servile."

The pause informed the boys they were to speak.

"Yes, Mr. Byrd."

"I leave you now with the words of our hospital anthem. *Blessed are they who considereth the poor.*"

Mr. Byrd bowed his head, both hands this time raised to his chin in prayer.

What did it all mean?

MARY 1877

What a Letter to Nan Might Say

It were a slow job, getting used to that great tall house, with sixty-four stairs from the kitchen to our attic, and water needing to be hauled to every room all the way up. The place were so strange, some days I'd be dizzy with wanting to be home. Only home weren't home anymore, what with Margaret Huckle being the queen hen, so I were stuck with putting one foot in front of the other to climb those steps.

Lord Allyn's newspapers were usually turned to kindling the day after, or wrapping for the fishbones, but I shredded *Monday, April 16,* through *Saturday, April 21,* stuffing a fine pillow, though it did rustle when I turned my head and Eliza made a point of sighing if she were still awake. We'd had real pillows in Pinchbeck, with sheep's wool or feathers inside, and quilts too; something I longed for now, with Eliza like a great sow, pulling the blanket over just herself more nights than not.

They'd been sending the heavy laundry out since the last girl were got rid of, but Eliza said Lady A. weren't happy with her linens being jumbled up with just anybody's. Who knew what infections might be lurking in the tubs at the laundress's? She'd heard about a washerwoman whose baby died of scarletina and there she were, using the same scrubbing board as she did for the sick child's bedding!

So my Mondays were determined by the carelessness of a grieving mother—or the story of one. Stories being what keeps the world spinning, while the daily tasks are ever the same. Every day were coal and water, trays and trolleys, sweeping and scrubbing, peeling, slicing, basting, serving. And each day of the week there were a big chore too: Mondays, laundry. Tuesdays, ironing. Wednesdays, turning the mattresses and changing the linens. Thursdays, Fridays, Saturdays . . .

Time slipped by, Lordy! I'd left Pinchbeck at the start of the year, and here it were coming into September already, though a city autumn were nothing like it appeared at home. First the Rogue and Scholar and then Neville Street had used up all those days. I'd had a birthday in July— secret to myself. On that day, I tore a bit of the butcher's paper into strips and fastened loops with a spot of paste from Cook's drawer, each loop linked through the next,

making a garland long enough to drape across the bed-
stead. It were very festive.

"And what's this for?" asked Eliza, tugging on it.

"Just a bit of cheering up," I said. She left it alone, and
I almost told her I'd turned fifteen, but then I didn't.

All that time gone and still some days my arms would
ache for wanting to hold Nan, before remembering she
were likely in that wriggly stage, squeaking to be put
down, and near big enough to have her hair braided. Did
her hair curl like Davy's? I wondered. Were she boister-
ous or sedate? Plump or scrawny? Were it a baby sister
she'd got or another brother? Did she remember me? Did
she love that Margaret Huckle instead?

I'd wish I could write her a letter. I'd think all day
sometimes, through all my tasks, telling her the news in
my head as if I could write it down. I'd report on the
sights, and think of funny stories, and imagine that
Thomas or Davy would read my words aloud in the
evening at the supper table, lit up by the lantern with
the dented tin lid.

Mrs. Wiggins? I'd say. *Well . . . Mrs. Wiggins's legs look
as if they've been poured into her stockings and settled
wrong, with swellings and lumps at odd spots. If I poked a
hole with the darning needle, or one of the skewers she
uses for the roast, we'd certainly see sand dribbling out
across the floor in a faint ribbon behind her.*

I could hear Nan giggling and I'd carry on. *You might
like to meet Nut,* I'd say, *and certainly your brothers would,*

him being everything we taught them not to be. He's an odd little chap, and most wouldn't notice him on the streets of London. He's small, of course, not having eaten his share of any meal since birth. Grubby little face, tough knuckles scabbed and ready for use. You see that look in his eyes and you're like to step out of his way rather than cross him.

Eliza says he arrived wearing a shirt must have belonged to a man twice his size, worn so thin you could count freckles through it.

It were Mrs. Wiggins asked Bates to fetch her a boy from the workhouse. "There's enough nasty jobs in any scullery to occupy a workhouse brat," Bates claims she said.

"Ha," says Nut to that. "There's nothing called a nasty job if'n you grew up in a workhouse."

He tells us tales sometimes, as fierce and fraidy as one of our dad's, only he says they're true. About the spiders he found crawling in the gruel, about how the spiders'd die after eating the gruel, about how the boys'd mash the spiders up and eat them to double their ration . . .

Oh? You want to know more about London? Well, I saw a bear on Saturday, yes I did! But I weren't afraid, because he were an old one and led on a chain, with a patchy pelt and moist eyes that looked more sad than hungry. The bear's boy were hanging about outside an alehouse. He'd got a whistle, blowing out a song without much music in it. The bear rose up to stand on his rear paws, sniffing and shifting his haunches till the whistle stopped. Some toff threw down a penny and the boy fed the bear a wee slice of meat before they ambled off to the next spot. It weren't so much, but I wish you'd seen it.

There's a cow, too, though that's nothing new to you. But here, in St. James's Park? You'll laugh when you hear, Nan. Fancy nursemaids bring children every day to line up and pay a penny for a cup of milk!

But wouldn't you rather taste something you've never tried? You could drink peppermint water, or coffee, or lemonade or ginger beer. If you're hungry, there's no end to the marvels being hollered about by hawkers and street vendors on every corner. Would you like to try pigs' feet? Or a rhubarb tart? Gingerbread? Hot eels? Plum cake? Oysters? A roasted corncob? Whelks? Pea soup?

Oh, but mentioning pea soup, I've got to say, you've never seen such a pea-soup fog as ladles itself over us in the afternoons. It's nothing like a bit of mist in the lane at home. The fog is so thick here it hides the gas jets in the street and you'd swear it's night, so thick you can almost swallow it.

"What are you thinking about, Mary Finn?" asked Eliza.

"Nothing really," I told her.

"Is your head so empty, Mary? You need a beau, so you can moon about him all day, instead of nothing."

I only wished I could write that letter. And receive one in return, telling me how Nan and our brothers were thriving. Our letter carrier had the name of Mr. Daniel. He were ever so smart-looking, in his scarlet coat and gold-banded hat. There were a time when I felt a little brighter hearing his double knock, meaning he'd put something in the box. If I were close by the door, I'd pop out and wave, and he'd wink and dash off, Eliza never missing the chance to tease, saying, "Ooh, Mary's got a soft spot for a man in uniform!"

I shushed her back then, but it turned out to be true, didn't it?

JAMES 1884

The First Night
Turned into Many Nights

Could it be only his first night? In the cot to his right was the freckly boy from the hair-cutting room. To the left was a slightly bigger boy with surprised-looking eyebrows. He'd been living there since summer, so he knew all there was to know, but not as much as Martin.

"My name is Frederick Mills," he announced. "Only not really. That's the stupid name they've given me and there's a better one that's mine."

"What do you mean?"

"Same for you," he said. "When you were a baby, they gave you a new name. What is it now? James? Don't you wonder what your *real* mother named you?"

"I . . . no," said James. Mama Peevey had called him Jamie. He was pleased with James, or Jamie. He hadn't thought much about being Nelligan instead of Peevey. It was a name, that was all. Was there something wrong with James?

"I'm just . . . James."

"Huh."

"Who named us?"

"Those gents downstairs. They don't even know us, and they made up names! I think all the time about who I really am. I'm pretty certain my father is . . . a prince, or possibly a famous general."

"My name is Walter," said the freckled boy. "Walter Raleigh."

Frederick laughed.

"What?" Walter hopped off his cot, fists up and ready. "Why should that be funny to you?"

"Only I wish it were mine," said Frederick, ignoring Walter's fists. "Do you even know who he was? Sir Walter Raleigh was a knight and an explorer. They've given you one of the best names!"

James looked at Walter with new eyes, hoping for sudden acts of daring. But Walter sat back down and put a thumb in his mouth.

"I want my mother," he said.

James thought of the row of mugs holding Fry's cocoa lined up on the painted table at home, Mama Peevey blowing on each of them so's there'd be no burned tongues.

"I do too," he said. He nearly put an arm around Walter's shoulder.

"Ah, forget home," said Frederick. "You're here now. Don't be babies. You're starting over. You'll stop thinking about them soon enough."

Not likely, thought James.

"There's more to worry about here than long-gone mothers."

"Like what?" said Walter.

"You keep sucking that thumb?" said Frederick. "They'll cut it off. Cut it right off, *phttt*"—he mimed a knife slicing down—"and feed it to the pigs."

Walter yanked his thumb out, his eyes welling up in the same moment.

"Baby." Frederick's mouth shaped a sneer.

James took a quick measurement. Pick your friends wisely, Mister had said. Did he want to be a baby?

"Feed it to us, more like," said James.

"What?" said Walter.

"What do you think that stew was made of? Boys' thumbs, that's what."

Walter made a squeaking little gasp as though James had pulled out a thumb saw. Fiercely, he shoved his hands under his bottom. Remorse tickled in James's throat.

"I'm teasing," he said. "It only tastes like thumbs."

He'd sniffed his chance at bossing, though, as delicious as a brown sugar tart. He suddenly knew he could get along by pretending to be Martin. As days went by, he tried swaggering, and even whispered Martin's naughty words for company.

"Devil's piss," he favored, and "God's bum." Or "damned," like "My damned bootlace just broke!" They were wicked words, but he said them quietly.

The new boys wore their nightshirts for two whole days until uniforms were assembled for them.

WHAT THEY WERE GIVEN TO WEAR:
- *White stockings, heels cobwebbed and toes bumpy with darning stitches*
- *Brand-new shoes! Leather stiff as wood, laces stiff as sticks*
- *White shirt, red waistcoat*
- *Brown knickers and jacket, made of thick and fuzzy wool*
- *Buttons, shiny brass, all six of them, like having coins sewn to their chests. Each button was engraved with a little lamb, the symbol of the Foundling Hospital. That lamb was pictured on the crockery too.*
- *Collar. This was possibly the silliest part, huge and round and forever flapping up.*
- *Necktie. And what was the purpose of a necktie, James wondered?*

That pimply boy who had taken away his clothes on the first day had worn all the same things. Oh, and a

- *Brown hat with red ribbon, for wearing out of doors*

James's fingers slipped under his cap many times a day, rubbing the soft, new bristles. Not Jamie's curls anymore. Nor James's, either. What was his real name? His trousers prickled, the jacket was too tight, the shoes were like *damned* cheese boxes strapped to his feet . . . but somehow there was comfort in rubbing a palm over the warmth of his scalp.

ELIZA 1877

Getting Sulky

Eliza had no complaint with Mary through the spring and summer, apart from her needing directing and reminding on certain points of being in service. The odd lot in the kitchen were actually chummy most times, if you could abide Nut's chatter, Mrs. Wiggins's spoffling at them to hurry up, and Bates being a moody blighter, only amorous when it suited him. Mary being a bit slow was nothing really. Only, the day come when it seemed to Eliza that Bates was a bit soft where Mary was concerned, and that made her sit up and take notice.

Mary was filling the hot-water jugs, to deliver them up to the bedrooms, so's the family could wash before dinner. She was telling the brat yet another story, with all the characters having the name Nut or Nutter or Nutty or some nonsense.

Mary acted out voices for the different people, so she growled when the wicked duke was talking. " 'Get down from that fine mare,' " said Mary. "The wicked duke threatened him with a sword. 'I'd like that horse in my own stable.' "

" 'It is not my horse to give,' said the loyal boy, Nuttwick. 'It belongs to Prince . . . Prince . . .' "

"Prince Nuttelberg," said Nut.

"If you say so," said Mary. She laughed as if it were a sweet, funny thing to say instead of his being pigheaded full of himself. " 'The horse belongs to Prince Nuttelberg, my lord.'

" 'All the more reason for me to have him,' growled the wicked duke. 'Dismount at once.' So the poor, loyal boy climbed down—"

"No!" said Nut. "He wouldn't do that! He would never climb down!"

"You're right," said Mary. "Whatever were I thinking? . . . The poor loyal boy sat taller in the saddle. 'No!' he cried, 'I'll never climb down, as long as I live and breathe!' "

Bates sat there, swishing the beer around in his mug, being the lord of the manor while Mrs. Wiggins had a "little lie-down," her being poorly. He did like to strut a bit whenever Cook hid herself.

"You know, Mary," he said, leaning back in his chair, tipping it up as would have had him scolded fierce if

Mrs. Wiggins were there. "It was me who brought Nut here from the workhouse."

Nut was hunched over, brushing the boots while he listened to Mary, but he looked up sharp when Bates said his name.

"Well, you picked a good boy, Mr. Bates," said Mary, and she tousled the brat's lousy hair like a mother would. Nut flattened it straight back down with his palm, smearing blacking across his forehead.

"Yes, I did," says Bates, "didn't I?" As if he'd had anything to do with the selection. "I walked into that place . . . and it was an awful place, I tell you. It ştank like a sailor's socks . . . and I thought to myself, 'If I can find one child, if I can help one boy pull himself up by his bootstraps . . .'"

"Funny as how you've never mentioned those fine feelings until today, Harry Bates," sulked Eliza. "Until certain persons was here to listen."

He threw a haughty look that stabbed a needle into her heart. "Some *certain persons* care to hear about *finer* feelings," he said. "While others are unduly concerned with more sordid cravings—"

Well, Eliza didn't wait around for more of that kind of talk. "Unduly, my *bottom*." She grasped two of the pitchers Mary had filled. "I'll take the jugs up," she muttered.

"Oh, you're taking the jugs up, all right," said Bates, ever so crass. And wouldn't you know? That loathsome Nut actually snickered.

JAMES 1884

Breakfast

James was hungry, wishing for toasted oatmeal bread with butter and apple jelly. The boys were marched into the dining hall while one of the masters struck a table with a mallet. *Tap. Tap. Tap.*

"Stay in time," Frederick had warned. "You get strapped otherwise." There were empty places at Frederick's table and James slid onto the bench.

"Don't sit down!" They were to wait for the mallet's signal. *T-tap.* "Now!" said Frederick.

Two hundred boys sat together. Another *tap.* Two hundred boys bowed their heads. James bowed his head but swiveled his eyes to know what should happen next. *T-tap.*

Two hundred boys spoke together. "Bless to me, O God,

what Thou hast provided for me, and give me grace to be thankful, through Jesus Christ my Savior."

Tap. Now there were murmurs and shuffling all around, spoons and forks fiddled with, salt scooped out of bowls and licked from palms.

"Where are the girls?" asked Walter.

"They live on the other side of the building," said Frederick. "Sometimes we see them in the yard, but we're not allowed to talk to them. Boys and girls together are sinners."

James did not have a chance to find out why, because the food arrived, bowls passed hand to hand along the table until each had one. James stared at a single ladleful of the thinnest *damned* gruel, nearly gray in color. He expected Mama Peevey to chuckle him awake and plonk down a bowl of real porridge, with top milk and some lumps in it. This watery dribble had barely enough grain to give it color, let alone lumps. But Frederick, and every other boy he could see, picked up his spoon and gobbled the muck down. James closed his eyes and thought about toast. The meal was over in less time than it had taken to march in and say the grace.

After breakfast they were gathered together to sit on stools in a classroom. Frederick had already told him they didn't have lessons until they were bigger. Instead, the youngest boys were taught to *do* things, like braid rope, or mend trousers, or make brooms.

On that first morning, a Big Chap called Tubbs stood

in front of them. Until now, James had seen only boys his own age, called Infants. But that word meant babies and James was *not* a baby.

"Some of you Infants have already tried this," said Tubbs. "So you know it's not as easy as it looks. They've picked me to show you because I'm best."

"He always says that," grumbled Frederick.

"Whatever rude thing you may be whispering," said Tubbs, "it will be a matter of blistering importance—you get that? *Blistering* importance"—he laughed at his own cleverness—"that you learn to darn a stocking properly. You want to know why?"

James nodded, caught up.

"Because all the hose goes—heh! That rhymes! All the *hose goes* into the same laundry tub, doesn't it? These stockings have been here since the first boys came, over one hundred years ago. They've been worn by stinking, fungusy feet, over and over and over. . . . So you won't necessarily be getting your own back, will you? You never know when your own *ittle toesies* will be inside a stocking that's been done wrong, do you? I'm here to teach you the battle cry: Hosiery need not be a misery! Now, watch carefully. . . ."

"He's a crackpot," whispered Frederick. "But scary."

"He's funny," said James, setting his sights higher than mere seven-year-old Frederick.

In his right hand, Tubbs held up a needle strung with wool. He plunged his left fist into the heel of a stocking, knuckles showing pink through threadbare patches.

James held his breath, not knowing what exactly he should be paying attention to. It looked complicated. Only moments later Tubbs had filled the holes with a neat latticework of white strands.

"Now it's your turn," said Tubbs, passing around a basket of limp white stockings. "Whatever you mend today, you'll wear tomorrow. That'll teach you better than anything."

James soon discovered he was a natural darner. Pulling the wool taut, but not so tight as to pucker what it was meant to be mending, gently weaving the blunt-tipped needle over and under, over and under . . . his breathing eased, his worry faded—he could do this!

Finished before any of the others, James couldn't help grinning as he held up the stocking. Wouldn't Mama Peevey think he was a clever boy? Tubbs's eyebrows lifted, faintly impressed.

"Good work. What's your name?"

"James," said James. "James Nelligan."

"Smell-Again, eh?" said Tubbs. James blinked. *Oh no, please not.*

"Excel-Again," said James, so quickly that he surprised himself. Frederick went still beside him. Tubbs snorted, but he handed another stocking to James and winked. *Ha,* thought James. *Devil's fart, but I'm clever.*

Holding On to Bates

She was a wily one, that Mary. Eliza had told her plain, hadn't she? She had set her sights on being Eliza Bates someday and Mary was to keep herself to herself as far as Bates was concerned.

It burnt a hole in Eliza's belly the way he'd perk up when Mary come into the kitchen or bent over to tinker with the fire. She *seemed* to pay him no mind, but Eliza wasn't fooled. You wouldn't think a young slip like that would have many tricks up her sleeve, but what other explanation could there be for Bates's wandering eye?

Eliza got her hopes up for a bit that Mary'd cotton on to Mr. Daniel, the letter carrier. She always jumped at his knock and prattled on so he'd have to drag himself off to finish his rounds. But wouldn't you know it? He had a wife!

The matter became urgent one morning when Mrs. Wiggins sent her out to the street with Bates, to help carry in a large order from the grocer. And to step lively.

"Hey, fella," said Eliza, quiet-like, holding a crate of beer. "I'll be counting linens at half past three. . . . What will you be doing?" She brushed past him closer than strictly needed. The linen cupboard was small and dark, with the advantage of blankets at hand to soften whichever hard surface might get bumped against during a tumbling.

"You'll be counting alone," said Bates, swinging a barrel of sugar up to his shoulder, jerking his chin to tell her *move over*.

"I could do it earlier," said Eliza, "Right after we've got the luncheon done?"

His head was shaking.

"Or later?"

"I'm busy, Eliza."

"Has Lady A. got you driving somewhere?"

"No."

"Tonight, then?" She hated herself for pushing.

"What the devil are you two doing?" Mrs. Wiggins waited in the doorway. "We need the sugar, Bates. Before Christmas."

"Not tonight," said Bates to Eliza.

She knew ahead what he'd be saying next, she knew it like she'd swallowed a spoon along with the pudding and it was choking her.

"I'll be taking a rest from counting linens," he said, calm as a priest. "I know how many there are."

"Taking a *rest?*"

Shut your mouth up, *Eliza,* she said to herself. He was cutting her off. She fought to keep the teasing smile on her face, not wanting to blub like a baby. She stepped in front of him with the beer bottles rattling, nearly treading on Mrs. Wiggins's swollen toes in her rush. Bates was right behind her. On usual days he'd have given her bottom a teasing pat.

Mary laughed somewhere in the pantry, calling Nut a greedy scamp. Eliza looked Harry Bates in the eye and saw it all. He wasn't counting linens with her because he was hoping to someday be counting linens with Mary. Eliza turned away so quick she felt her neck crink. It hadn't happened yet, she knew that much. There must be something she could do.

JAMES 1884

The Routine and the Corpse

It was all new to James, not possibly imagined, mostly awful. He'd never tasted such terrible food. His clothes were scratchy, forcing his legs and arms to struggle in woolen bindings. Since that first scalding bath, there'd been nothing but cold water for washing in. The ward where he slept—tried to sleep—was enormous and drafty, with a scary night nurse or matron stationed at each end. But even the matron did not prevent the bullies from pouncing.

Each evening, after supper and prayers, a few of the Big Chaps—ten or eleven years old, some of them—were enlisted to wash the smaller ones. Shivering in his nightshirt, James learned the ritual.

GETTING WASHED:

- *Line up in bare feet, on stone floor like a winter doorstep*
- *Put hands out, palms together*
- *Big Chap slaps cloth soaked in icy water around hands*
- *Keep hands out, palms facing up*
- *Big Chap slaps cloth soaked in icy water across palms*
- *Turn to go, pray for mercy*
- *Big Chap cracks cloth soaked in icy water against backs of knees, causing snapping pain*
- *Don't cry, don't stumble*
- *All clean*

By Saturday, the routine was too familiar. Was it better to know what to expect, or was he hoping for something new?

"It'll be your first Sunday tomorrow, won't it?" said Frederick as they waited in line. It was Tubbs and Ben Franklin and Harvey Hooper manning the basins and wielding the cloths. James recognized that note of I-know-something-you-don't-know in Frederick's question. Yes, it would be his first Sunday. Could things get worse?

"What's going to happen?" asked Walter, thumb hovering at his lip.

"Hey, Tubbs!" called Frederick. "First Sunday for these ones. Don't you want to tell them?" He bounced and giggled. "Are you afraid of the dark, Sir Walter Raleigh?"

Harvey Hooper squeezed a cloth over Frederick's head, the gush of water making him squeal.

"You," said Tubbs, poking Frederick. "You. Need. To. Shut. Your. Worm-smelling. Mouth."

A thin sigh escaped from Walter, sagging as he watched.

Yes, thought James. Things could get worse. But *how* exactly?

These were only middle-sized Big Chaps. James had noticed that the very big ones—the thirteen- and fourteen-year-olds who were almost apprentices, or going to be trained up as sailors and soldiers—they didn't bother with new boys.

But these fellows had something to prove to each other. These were like those gang boys at home, who shouted rude things, and once broke the Peeveys' shop window and took all the biscuits they could reach through the jagged-edged smash.

James pretended not to notice the grins between the Big Chaps. In less than a week he'd learned to *seem* not to notice anything. It was safest with Big Chaps to see nothing and be nobody.

On Saturday night, Nurse Lees (known as Breath-Like-Old-Cheese) extinguished the lamps and hobbled off with her lantern to patrol the west wing dormitories. In the shadowy gloom, James found four boys plunking heavily onto his cot. Five, if he counted the squeaking, wriggling Walter dropped there by the others.

"Are you afraid of the dark?" It was Tubbs asking, but James could hear Frederick creaking the planks of his cot.

"Don't hurt us," said Walter.

"I love the dark," lied James.

"Then it won't bother you when we take you down to the crypt under the chapel," said Tubbs.

James considered.

"It'll bother you, all right," put in Frederick. "It's gruesome!" But then Harvey cuffed him and Walter moaned, while James thought about what to say.

"Why?" he asked.

"That's where the coffin—" Frederick started, before getting hit again.

Coffin?

"C-c-coffin?" said Walter.

"There's a curse," said Monty. "Coram's Curse."

"Don't tell us!" shrieked Walter. "I don't want to hear!"

Harvey plastered his palm over Walter's mouth and kneaded his ear as if it were bread to be served at breakfast. Walter's eyes bulged while his head twisted in panic.

"One more noise and your tongue is coming out," said Harvey. "Listen carefully, because you have to learn the curse if you don't want it to come true."

"Walter will listen," said James. "Won't you, Walter? You just were playacting, weren't you?"

"No," sniffed Walter. "What are they going to do to us?"

"Just listen, you stupid baby," said Ben Franklin. "You know who Thomas Coram is, right? The fellow who had the grand idea of saving stupid babies like you from starving to death in the streets? He got the king to give him money—"

"There isn't a king," said Walter. "It's Queen Victoria."

"It was a king *then*," said Tubbs. "And Thomas Coram, he started this hospital and then he hung about, wearing an old red coat and passing out gingerbread to stupid babies until he died."

"He died a horrible, lonely death," said Ben, his voice lower and shakier than before. "In a tiny, dirty room, with his mattress covered in spiders. And he had no friends coming to visit."

"And then," said Tubbs, "he was buried . . . only not actually *buried underground,* because his coffin . . . with his body inside . . . the coffin is on a slab in the vault. . . ."

"And," whispered Harvey, "the lid of his coffin—because the rats have chewed it—the lid doesn't fit quite properly—"

Frederick giggled and Tubbs pinched him.

"The lid is crooked . . . ," said Harvey. "And his *hand* is sticking out . . . the long, bony *fingers* are dangling over the edge of the box. His ghost wants company and he's . . . always *beckoning.* . . ."

Walter whimpered.

"Coram's Curse," began Tubbs, in an ominous drone, and then recited the poem in the most dreadful voice.

"Every child who comes this way
Must visit Coram first Sunday.
In his coffin, there he lies;
Tattered coat and hollow eyes.

Below the chapel, *far* below,
Through the darkness you must go.
Find him, see him, *touch his bones,*
Or you shall surely die alone . . ."

James couldn't help shivering. He knew the Big Chaps were trying to be scary . . . but he didn't quite believe they'd *hurt* him. And huddled on his bed in the dark with older boys all around? It was almost like being at Martin's house with his noisy, bothersome brothers. It was almost like having friends.

MARY 1877

Telling About the First Encounter

We scurried down Arthur Street, Eliza pulling on my hand while I banged into people left and right with the basket, suffering their curses and scowls without her heeding any of it, she were so bent on her endeavor.

"Oh, can't you hurry!" she scolded. "We mustn't be gone any more time than it takes to buy a fish!"

"The fish mar . . . ket . . . is the . . . other way," I puffed. "Covent Gar . . . den, is it not . . . ?" I pointed over my shoulder.

"Of course it is, you ninny! That's why we're running! We'll circle back that way. But you must see, you'll—"

We rounded the corner and the reason for Eliza's tizzy were clear at once. Forty men or more, in one small street; sitting about, leaning on walls, smoking, laughing, brushing horses, polishing boots, spitting, cursing, and generally strutting their manly selves.

"What—?"

I began to skitter backward but Eliza gripped me as a pair of tongs grips a cutlet.

"There's a barracks here," she whispered. "It's a girl's dream come true!"

"No, Eliza, not me." I were blushing already, guessing the kind of girl who might dream that way!

I were surprised at the gall of her. Under usual circumstances, Eliza thought of one man only and his name were Bates. But even with him, she complained when he took his jacket off in company, if you can call us in the kitchen company. Yet here she were, gawping at a crowd of *dozens,* and these men were not entirely·clad. Indeed, several lolled about without shirts at all!

"Eliza! We should not be here!"

I yanked my hand from hers and turned to flee, but at that moment saw an urchin, smaller and much dirtier than Nut. His grimy fingers closed around Eliza's purse and gave a mighty yank, us being otherwise distracted.

"Stop!" I cried. "Stop, you! Hey!"

Eliza spun about, thinking it were me who pulled on her. Seeing the boy, she screamed, tripped, and fell forward over her own clodhoppery feet, landing on the muddy cobbles with a *thunk* and a moan. I stared at her upended bottom and missed snatching at the boy.

All about us now were *men,* utterly confusing the

situation. They tried to right Eliza and each report what he had seen, each clamoring to say the most.

I held Eliza's arm and tried to wipe away the mud.

"My purse!" she sobbed. "I shall be whipped—"

"Not whipped, Eliza," I muttered. "Surely not whipped."

"Whipped!" she wailed. "Alack this day!"

It were not until the word *alack* that I saw her game. She shook free my hold to accept assistance from the whole company of men around us.

If she had seen herself in a glass, she'd have delayed her drama, for she were smeared with mud and horse dung from hem to cap, with her nose blazing scarlet to match the men's jackets.

"It was my lady's money!" explained Eliza, to the few men who listened still.

I'm not proud to say, but a giggle tickled at my throat, so I looked away while she flirted. I stood on tippy-toe, though I had no hope of spying the boy, who would be vanished and cheering his luck by now.

But then, up went a cry.

"What? Tucker?"

"Tucker's got it!"

"He caught the brat and trounced him!"

"Is it true?" I asked, pulling on the sleeve of the nearest soldier. Eliza paused in her performance.

A grinning lad approached, holding high a muddy prize that were the stolen purse. He were nearly as bespattered as Eliza, but his comrades clapped him on the shoulders as he passed and set up a chant in jest, "Tucker! Tucker! Tucker!"

He put the purse in Eliza's outstretched hand and then bowed low and clicked his heels, causing huge hilarity amongst the others. Now that he were near, we could see that he were closer to boyhood than most of them and dressed in the fashion of a groom, not the full uniform of the Coventry Guard.

"Caden Tucker, at your service." He ignored the friendly jeers.

As Eliza's mouth still hung open, I had the wits to bob.

"We thank you, kind sir," I said, matching his elegance. "This is Eliza Pigeon, whose whipping you have averted, and who will speak again when she has caught her breath."

I pinched her, and she blurted, "Aye!"

Caden Tucker now turned his eyes to me, and sure I felt the crackling blue heat of them, alongside a glimpse of a cheeky smile and a head full of shining dark curls, not that I were thinking so poetic at the moment.

"And you?" he asked.

Eliza began to moan about the state of her dress and tried to wipe it with her hands, which only moved the muck around. The men had lost interest and were wandering back to their boot polishing and arm wrestling and tobacco chewing.

"I'm Mary, sir. Mary Finn." I bobbed a second time. "We were meant to be buying fish, but got waylaid. . . ." I tugged Eliza's arm. "Come on, we'll catch it something terrible now."

She let me lead her just a step before she winced and bleated, grabbing at Caden Tucker as she stumbled.

"How far are you from home?" he asked.

"We live in Neville Street," I told him.

"I could walk with you for a bit," he said.

"Oh, would you?" Eliza leaned on his arm. "I feel a weakness in my knee and a terrible pain about the ankle."

This time I saw her plan as clear as Mr. Tucker's blue eyes. "Rot," I muttered. She screwed up her mouth at me, though not so's he could see it.

But then a drum were banged in the alley where the men lingered and Mr. Tucker were instantly at attention, as if prodded with a stick, along with every man in sight.

"I'm sorry," he said, rapidly straightening and attempting to brush himself off. He were gone before we could reply, and Eliza's mouth were still open.

"You are not truly injured?" I asked as nicely as I could.

"Me? I'm right as rain," she said. "But we haven't got the fish!"

"It's a lucky thing you landed in mud. We can tell the truth about what happened, and just not mention where."

Eliza smiled at me. "That's good," she said. "But did you tell him the *number* of the house on Neville Street?"

"What?"

"You must confess," she said with a sigh, "it worked out perfectly! And he very nearly walked us home! Was he not the *handsomest* boy?"

His laughing eyes darted across my mind.

I glared at her. "Eliza!"

"He liked you, too, I think," she said.

"Shall I go alone to fetch the fish?"

"No, no!" she said. "You must come back with me and tell Mrs. Wiggins how we nearly lost the purse."

Eliza bore her scolding with surprising good humor. We were pronounced useless and Bates were sent to the shops. He commenced to scowling and spluttering, such an errand being so far beneath him.

"I could go," offered Nut.

"Ha," said Bates, pulling on his boots. "No point sending out another one who'll not get what's wanted."

"Oh, I'd say we got exactly what was wanted," murmured Eliza, with a saucy wink at me.

OLIVER 1884

History

As dry as dead bugs, was how the students might catego-
rize Oliver Chester. He knew that. They called him Fester
Chester or Blister Chester, somewhat uncreatively, he
thought. It had been the same in his day, coming up with
rhyming or alliterative nicknames for the masters and matrons. Full-of-Snot Aldercott had arrived when he was in
the fifth form. Only the good Lord knew how old she must
be by now!

Oliver included Captain Thomas Coram in the lesson
about King George II, as an example of persistence paying off. He'd tell how the sea merchant had petitioned the
king for seventeen years before convincing him to grant
the charter to start the Foundling Hospital. They all knew
about the charter, as Charter Day dinner was the one time

apart from Christmas when they could depend on having dessert.

Oliver would describe Captain Coram's daily walk past the dung heap where he witnessed dying babies and conceived the idea of a home to care for abandoned children. Dung and dying babies were certain to absorb them. But, thanks to the legend of the crypt, passed down through the generations, the boys were well acquainted with Coram's ghost and did not care a plate of figs for tales of the real man.

As a five-year-old, nearly thirty years ago, Oliver had narrowly dodged pissing in his pants during his own initiation. Now he occasionally slipped down to the chapel on Saturdays following Reception Day, telling himself he was keeping an eye out for misdoings. But truly? Those nights were rare spots of fun for Oliver, watching his childhood from afar.

Oliver waited for the creaking and whispering to pass along the corridor before he followed, not quite on tiptoe, but putting his feet down carefully, softly, to avoid dull scuffing on stone. He skated in the near-dark across the chapel floor, sliding into a back pew with a clear view of the stairway that led down to the crypt.

There were four Big Chaps, as far as Oliver could make out. They sat on the top step goading four or five new boys into creeping down to where nightmares were inevitable. The single candle stayed at the top, causing ghastly shadows to flit against the walls like prehistoric moths. The smallest boy was already shaking with sobs.

Oliver, bent low to remain secret, sternly asked himself a question, not for the first time. Was he behaving indecently by not stepping in at once? Or was he allowing the boys a rare moment to be something other than little tin soldiers?

"It's too dark down here!" More than one of them was wailing now.

"Stay where you are, you stupid babies."

"And don't come out without fetching a bone from Coram's coffin."

Time for Oliver's favorite interlude. With his lips closed, he began to moan far back in his throat. A hum, but the gloomy hum of a dying man.

The Big Chaps were startled to attention, shifting their eyes, flexing their fists.

"Do you hear that?"

"What the *hell* is that?"

A scream tore up from below, the candle fell and was extinguished. The Big Chaps bumped into one another in the scramble. The noise was so fearful that Oliver stopped his nonsense and stepped out of hiding.

Three small boys in nightshirts raced up the stairs, faces wild and breathing ragged. Behind them came a creature, another white-clad boy, of course, but his skin was smeared and his hair was spiky with gray dust. His hands formed swiping claws and he released a piercing shriek that sent the whole pack running—straight into Mr. Chester.

"Aaaaaahh!" Worse even than an apparition was the sight of the history master finding them out of the ward at half past ten at night.

"Settle down, boys." Oliver waited. "Hooper. Franklin. Tubman."

"Sir."

"Yes, sir."

"Sir."

"Correct me if I am mistaken. Your purpose here is to frighten children."

They hung their heads while the smaller boys finished up whimpering. Oliver turned to them.

"I am Mr. Chester. I teach history and will meet all you boys in a couple of years. One of the things you will learn during your history lessons is how wrongdoers in the past have been punished. Isn't that right, Franklin?"

"Yes, sir."

"In his coffin, eh? There he lies . . . Tattered coat and hollow eyes?"

"Yes, sir."

Oliver looked down at the huddle of new ones.

"A phantom seems to have come up with you from the crypt."

The dusty boy grinned and made claws again. Very plucky.

"What's your name?"

"Nelligan, sir. James Nelligan."

"Well then, Nelligan—"

Someone snickered.

"What did you think of the crypt?"

"Uh, cold, sir."

"Why don't you tell us how these wrongdoers should be punished? Solitary confinement? Guillotine? One hundred lashes on a bare back?"

"They should go down in the crypt, sir. For an hour. Alone. At night."

"That's a jolly good idea."

MARY 1877

Telling About Sweets

It were a pleasure to scrub the steps on a sunny morning in October, when we'd lost the smell of summer. To have a bright blue sky were a surprise, a present out of season, as if we could have strawberries at Christmas. I swept the steps every day, of course, first thing before starting the rooms, cinders and soot piling up in the corners almost as quick as sneezing. But whiting I used only once a week.

The sun were pale and low that day, warm, like someone's pipe resting, or a new wool chemise. I were aching to be outside, wishing for a garden or the lane, but settling for the steps instead.

I said aloud in the kitchen, "I'd best white those steps this morning. The sun will do half the work." I gathered up bucket and brush and went out to have fifteen minutes of that warmth across my shoulders.

This were only two days after Eliza's purse were swiped and you'll soon see how Mr. Caden Tucker had latched on to me saying "Neville Street" with both his ears. But at the time, I were startled, me being in a position that no girl likes a young man to find her in, backside to the street, skirts hooked up and sleeves rolled back to the elbow, in the unlikely chance of keeping the cuffs dry.

He were there a moment before I turned around. A shadow paused and I thought nothing until it lingered. I looked around and *Dammit!* went right across my mind. Yes, it did, *Dammit,* me looking particular unsightly. But he didn't smirk or sneer or say any of the cheeky things that Bates would have said, did say usually.

"Why do you start at the bottom and work up to the top?" he asked, seeming truly curious. "Why not the other way, so the dirty water drips onto the dirty stone instead of the clean?"

"I ... I ... it were the way Eliza showed me," I said, finally. "We never had steps, at home. But your way makes more sense, I see that."

He grinned and my ribs creaked in their effort to hold the heart's flutter. *Oh Lordy no,* I thought, *don't go falling for a young man only on account of dark curls and blue eyes.*

I worried my face were blazing, what with bending over and having the sun on me and sweating and being flustered all in the same minute. I bent back down, only then my bottom would be stuck up in his face, wouldn't it? So I had to kneel and the steps were wet and my skirt got sodden at once. I felt such a lummox, making a bad job worse.

But he were gazing up at the house, instead of at me.

"Neville Street." He were smooth as new butter. "I thought you'd said Neville, and here you are."

Now the blush tore up my neck and across my cheeks like fire catching paper.

"Number eleven." He grinned again, and the sun did shine a little hotter, I swear.

"So," he said. "Now I know."

"That you do," I said, scrambling not to be a stammery ninny. "And what'll you do with such valuable information?" Fancy me being so sassy!

"I'll know how far a pretty girl might need to walk to meet someone Thursday next at half past seven by the main gate to Russell Square."

Cheeky bugger!

"Good day." And he sauntered off with me watching his back, not thinking of a single clever word to say.

But then he stopped and spun around and caught me looking! If I were pink before, now I were the scarlet of a postman's uniform. I closely examined the scrubbing brush, as if it were misbehaving.

But he weren't tricking me on purpose, to tease. He came back to ask, "Are you fond of peppermints?"

"I'm not . . . I haven't . . . I wouldn't know," I mumbled.

"Well, that's a situation must be corrected this very day," he said, and winked! Leaving me to lean against the railing, waiting for breath to reenter my body.

I won't pretend I didn't think about him every minute that whole day long. But it weren't until we'd served up-stairs and were having our own supper that I knew I'd not been dreaming. Mrs. Wiggins sent Eliza to the cellar for a new jar of pickles, she being particular partial to having pickles with her mutton. There came a quick double rap on the kitchen door.

Mrs. Wiggins clapped a hand to her bosom. "Whoever can that . . . ? At this hour?" She motioned Nut to answer. We all could see that no one were there, but Nut scooped something from the ground and came back with a little paper cone, twisted closed, that had a note on it.

Bates leaned over. "It says *Mary*." He plucked the packet out of Nut's fist and gave it a sniff.

"Peppermint." He raised an eyebrow. "Or should I say, the scent of a young man lurking?"

I knew already, not being a fool. Not being a fool, I didn't grab for it either. I raised up some quizzical eye-brows myself and managed a shrug, while my mouth were fighting to laugh and my feet were wishing to skip a bit of a reel.

"Mr. Bates," scolded Mrs. Wiggins. "Not in my kitchen, if you please. And Mary? If you've got yourself a young man, you can get yourself rid of him as well. We've got rules here."

Bates laughed, likely thinking of breaking those rules with Eliza.

"That'll be enough of that." Mrs. Wiggins were firm with him, the only one who could be. "Give Mary what's hers and leave it to me to talk sense to the girl."

Bates bowed and put the little twist on the table next to me. Eliza came up from the cellar just then, one hand holding BREAD AND BUTTER, the other holding DILLED.

She glanced at Bates and gave the packet a bit of a glare, reminding me I wouldn't be telling her, either, where the sweets came from, not giving her the satisfaction after all her hints and nonsense.

Eliza were staring at me, as were Nut, Mrs. Wiggins, and Bates. We finished the meal in utter silence. More of us than me, I am certain, were considering how a paper cone of candy might change my life.

ELIZA 1877

Getting Fed Up

Eliza thought she might grind her own teeth to splinters by the end of that supper. Him giving her sweets out in front of everyone, that was as ill-mannered and hurtful as a fellow could think of. And nobody making so much as a comment of consolation to her after?

Resentment itched Eliza. After her teaching Mary to be a proper tweenie—a maid between stairs, meaning up and down and everywhere in between . . . covering her mistakes, of which there were plenty she could think of . . . Imagine! Going at the grates without gloves! All the laundry lessons, all the nights in the same iron-posted bed . . . Eliza wished Mary would have the courtesy to explain, or apologize, or *flaunt* even, so there'd be a natural reason to tear at her hair until it ripped right out.

But to pretend the moment hadn't happened? That just burned Eliza's bonnet, that did.

Remember the Forsaken Poor

James felt clever on Saturday night in the chapel, but come Sunday morning on the same spot, he didn't feel so clever anymore. On Saturday night, Mr. Chester had polished his round spectacles on his waistcoat and smiled at James with his crooked mouth before sending the bullies to the crypt and the little boys back to their beds.

On Sunday morning, however, it was the Big Chaps who surrounded him before the service began.

"You will pay for the rest of your days."

That was what Tubbs said in James's ear, digging his knuckles deep into James's neck. Harvey Hooper rammed his hand under James's collar and let loose a fistful of salt, saved especially from the breakfast table.

Those thick, tall boys slid away right quick. Quick as snakes, all gone. James saw why, with Mr. Byrd's eyes watching and Mr. Florence, the choirmaster, waiting. All the masters stood in a special place, with the lady teachers from the girls' side too. Mr. Chester was there, but too far away to notice that those same menacing Big Chaps were at it again.

James and the other Infants sat in the front row where he could mostly see only railing. The bench was hard. The boys behind must have had fire in their eyes because the heat on James's neck was most distracting. The boys behind were supposed to tell a master if any small foundling moved one bit during chapel. His eyeballs ached from holding in misery. He counted curses for distraction.

Devil's fart.

God's bum.

He needed a new one. Or two. Something to do with . . .

Coram! Coram's skull!

Coram's breath . . . Yes, the crypt could supply an endless list!

But then Mr. Florence tapped a stick on his music stand and the choir began to sing. There was a rush of air in James's ears like the whole huge chapel was fluttering with a thousand birds. His ears flew up higher and higher and he forgot to breathe. He looked at the other boys to see if they were marveling as he was, or if he was the only one who'd never heard such songs before. That was an hour he would remember, probably forever.

The next hour too, but for a different reason.

They lined up like always outside the boys' refectory.

They each were wearing a new Sunday collar, which James already hated; stiff, tickling thing.

They marched slowly into the dining hall, in time with the striking mallet. James went to his place and stood behind the bench. This part he already knew. But today, Sunday, there were strangers clustered near the walls. Some of the gentlemen kept their hats on and some held them under their arms. The ladies wore dresses in beautiful colors, like a row of biscuit tins with pretty labels.

Like the tins in the Peeveys' shop.

The mallet rapped. James bowed his head and clasped his hands in front, as all the others did. *Rap!* He closed his eyes and listened to one of the Big Chaps—which one? He opened one eye and tried to see without turning his head. It was Monty Clemens, who had carroty hair, even under his arms, according to Frederick. Monty said the grace, using words fast.

"Father of mercies, by whose love abounding all we Thy creatures are sustained and fed, may we while here on earth Thy praises sounding, up to Thy heavenly courts with joy be led."

The servers carved roast beef and spooned out boiled greens. James held on to both sides of his plate, sniffing, hopeful. Maybe food tasted better on Sundays. There seemed to be more of it. The visitors began to move between the tables, pointing at the food and looking closely at the boys. Was he supposed to stop and look at them? No, the others were ignoring the waving and watching.

They were just eating. James just ate, though his throat was clogged.

Some of the spectators said things.

"Fancy giving beef to charity children!" That was a lady with blue gloves, holding a man's arm.

"No wonder they gobble it up like goats," said the man.

James shut his eyes and tried to chew loudly enough not to hear the talking.

"The boy who spoke the grace," one lady said. "With the red hair? You can see his mother was an Irish slut!" That made laughter ripple around.

James kicked Frederick's ankle, not hard, just to get his attention.

"What?" said Frederick.

"Why are they here?" whispered James.

"They come to see us," said Frederick. "Sometimes they give us pennies."

"But *why*?"

"Because we're poor."

"Poor," said James. "Not deaf."

A lady wearing a violet dress swished along their row. She leaned over with her gray bonnet right next to James's face. Close enough that he could have bitten off one of the silky little rosebuds on the hat's brim. Her nose was bumpy but her eyes were soft brown and worried-looking. James stopped chewing. You can't chew or swallow when someone's bumpy nose is nearly touching yours.

"Hello," she said. "Aren't you a pretty one!"

Frederick made a rude noise and pretended it was a cough. The lady kept peering at James. The stupid collar was going to choke him. He lowered his eyes, awkward with staring.

"Ohh! The lashes!"

Frederick snorted again. James booted him. He felt roast beef in his throat, mixed with the smell of the lady, which made him think of cake. He might be sick, he really might. Two Big Chaps watched from the other side of the table.

"Are you new, dear?" asked the lady. "I don't think I've seen you before."

"Yes, he's new," said one of the older boys. "He doesn't talk much, but he likes pennies."

James flinched. "I do not!" Of course he did, really, but it was bad manners to say so!

The lady smiled, showing edges of buckteeth and crinkling her friendly eyes. "I am Lady Bellwood," she said. "What is your name?"

Frederick booted him this time.

"James," he whispered.

"Hello, James. You little dear." She opened her purse and tucked something from her hand into his. "That's for you, mind, not for those other boys." And she *winked*.

Her skirt was twisted by the bench leg when she tried to stand up but she got free and went away. James slid his fist below the table to glimpse his prize: three sweets wrapped in waxy paper.

"What've you got there?" Ben Franklin was quick. James pushed two candies into his cuff before his hand was jerked into view.

"Give it to me!" Ben snatched the sweet.

James grabbed at him but mostly for show. He wasn't going to fight with Ben Franklin. He only wanted Sunday dinner to be over and never come again.

Visitors

When Oliver was a boy, spectators had been permitted into the wards at night to observe sleeping foundlings. He wondered whether they hadn't even been *encouraged* to visit, on the chance that a potential benefactor's heart might be swayed by the sight of a stray curl resting against a slumbering cheek . . .

He'd had a naughty streak, even he would admit that, as dry and sensible as the boys might think him now. He and Rawson Smith had planned many an entertainment for the denizens of Ward Three. It had begun honestly enough, when Oliver awoke one night, with a total stranger sitting on his bed, rearranging his blanket. He'd screamed. Who wouldn't? He'd startled the woman, the matron, and the whole dormitory full of boys. The next time, Rawson did it on purpose, with the same prolonged effect on the audience. The time after that, Oliver added moaning, and a few twitches, before rolling himself off the edge of the bed. Rawson then sat up in terror, grabbing the skirt of a tiptoeing lady visitor, claiming he'd dreamt of Death wearing a cape. The final event had involved a boiled beet, carefully saved from dinner. Oliver remembered the sharp-tasting juice sitting in his mouth while he'd waited to leak "blood" during the evening tour . . .

That had been the end of it. Oliver and Rawson were caned and wrote five hundred lines each: *I will not create false nightmares but will instead accept God's mercy to the forsaken poor.*

Night visiting had soon after been terminated.

MARY 1877

Telling About the Letter

The day came when Mr. Daniel knocked twice and were standing there still when I'd wiped the carrot shreds off my hands to open the door. He handed me a small bundle of letters but kept one apart.

"This one is for you, Mary."

I suppose he didn't expect me to know my letters. He pointed to where my name were writ out, bold and square.

Did he notice my upset? "It may not be bad news," he said, quiet-like, trying to reassure me. "Bates can read. And Eliza. Take it to the table." He nudged me across the stoop and waited. Finally, he closed the door for me. I were that shook, wondering what calamity I held there, feeling the paper under my thumbs until it warmed.

I'll give Bates credit that his voice changed as he read.

To Mary Finn,

My sister Fanny wrote to us that you ran away, which news has broken your father's heart. We received word from you also, writ by your friend, but it did not balance our disappointment. We wonder that a girl so young should be so headstrong. For the safety of the children you are not welcome here again.

You now have a half sister, Phoebe, born May 12, 1877, and another one coming, though it shames me that you are related by blood.

We all are well here in Pinchbeck, except your brother John, who passed from this earth on the 10th of September. He is buried next to your mother, Mary Ann Boothby Finn.

Your father asked me to write.
                                        Sincerely,
                                        Margaret Finn

I tore the paper from Bates's hand. Margaret *Finn*? How dare she? Small John, dead and buried? I slid into the chair, instantly swallowed by the shock. I shook off whosever hand touched my back, my face hidden while I wept for my dear brown-eyed boy. It were certainly that cough that took him and I blamed Margaret Huckle for not knowing about chest plasters or bowls of steam or spoonfuls of honey before bed. But worse, letting myself be sent off made it my fault, and then going further away instead of home. I cringed, remembering Mam, her littlest boy lost on account of me.

The bell jangled above our heads, from the library.

"They'll be wanting their tea," said Mrs. Wiggins. "You've had your cry. Now splash your face and get on with it. Take the post up too."

I were sniffing and bubbling when I lifted my head to see all their faces turned elsewhere, giving me that whole minute to mourn my baby brother. Nut slid his hand under mine, setting me off again. But I upped and put on clean cuffs, changed my apron, and took the tea tray to the library. I put it down on the nice doily that lay over the table by the window.

"Thank you, Mary," said Lady Allyn, barely smiling. At the desk, Lord A. kept moving his pen, not looking up. Neither of them had half a care for me, even if they'd known that my brother had died. I backed out of the room that held all those prized books, all the words written by men who'd got servants bringing tea and not one of them thinking how it mattered that I had spooned honey into Small John's fevered mouth, or mended his blue jacket, or been proud of him picking out the letters on a grave-stone.

Somehow I knew there were a gulch between what got writ down about history and what were remembered by the people who went along living it. No doubt the scholars checked their facts about battles and such non-sense, but weren't those battles fought by boys who'd wished for their mams, or bought peppermints or arm wrestled to win a bit of tobacco? Days went by, girls left home, children died, and who marked it all?

JAMES 1888

Finds the Tree

James didn't think of climbing the tree until he was nearly ten years old and being chased by Harvey Hooper for the purpose of having his "poxy little mongrel's face pushed in."

"Touch me and *you'll* get the pox!" he'd shouted, but that idea didn't have much plunk with a brain the size of Harvey's.

Until that day, James had often hidden behind one tree or another, but had never considered climbing. One hand on the bark, ready to slip between the tree and the wall, he happened to glance up, and had an instant of soaring recollection—of Mister's strong hands clasping his waist, lifting him high enough to catch hold of the lowest branch.

James leapt, and surprised himself by being able to

reach, just as Harvey's voice called out, "Nelligan, I'll get you, wherever you've hid your ugly face." James grinned, palms smarting, feet scrambling till they suddenly found a spot and he was safe. The next branch was hardly higher, an easy climb. He watched the yard, spying on Harvey's confused face and stomping-away boots. James shifted his wedged bottom, and— Coram's ghost! He could see right over the wall and into the street!

Oh, the hubbub! What that narrow brick wall had been hiding! James stretched out along the branch—that day, and whenever he could afterward—watching the wild world outside from the safety of his perch.

The tree gave James a new life, a room to himself, the crow's nest on a sailing ship overlooking the Outside. His branch was higher than anywhere he'd ever been in an outdoors place, perhaps as high as the dormitory windows. The light was different under there, pretty and lacy, always shifting as leaves fluttered, a perfect green curtain. He couldn't go every day, not even every week, but sneaking up there was even better than sitting at history lessons. It was the Now part of history, thought James. His breath came fast as he climbed each time, knowing there'd be . . . something *different* to see. At the Foundling, every minute could be predicted and accounted for. The Outside was so busy and crowded that James could never predict or account, much as he'd tried. No list could ever capture it all.

His view of that stretch of street (which street was it? He wished he knew its name) became his secret source of knowledge, like finding a book written in a language that none of the other boys could understand. And he'd certainly never show them.

As he lay up there, twitching and giddy, poked by rough tree knobs, James tried to memorize everything, to tell all the things for sale to Mama Peevey that never were in the shop at home.

- *Pies!*
- *Every kind of flower, also watercress in baskets*
- *Milk and beer and pressed lemon drink*
- *Mattresses!*
- *Lots of slimy things that looked, from where James lay, like slugs in little saucers: mussels, they were called, or oysters*
- *There was a fellow sometimes passing who bought hair— yes, hair. He'd cut the length from a girl's head and pay her something for it. What did he do with it? James could never tell.*

Oh, it was too much to think about while watching! He wanted to save some for later, like the sweets that Lady Bellwood and the other lady visitors gave to him on Sundays.

MARY 1877

Love

I suppose you'll think I'm a right hussy when I tell you we got to kissing the third time I ever saw him. I will only say that it were soon after I had the letter from Margaret Huckle and I were oddly jumpy. There were something tingling inside, making me laugh when I ought to be crying, making me notice the colors or the taste of things. The rules were not sitting so firm in my mind.

You'll remember that Caden Tucker had given notice as to where he might be loitering at a certain time, should I happen to be there too. I had been worrying since morning what reason to use, but then a gift were presented, in the shape of Master Sebastian's emerging teeth. This were his second time to alter my life's bumpy path, and he just eight months old. As Mam would say, this leading to that, the history of a person could be so directed by the incidental nub of a tooth chafing its way through.

The baby's fussing were a wish come true. Before tea I were sent to fetch gripe water, ready-made, and oil of clove from the chemist, though I could have certainly mixed up my own, as my brothers and sister would tell you.

I made the purchase and slipped it into my apron pocket. I pulled my shawl tighter round me, seeing the torches being lit against the fog.

"Have you got it?" asked Miss Hollow, who were waiting in the kitchen, tapping her pointed little boot.

"No, ma'am." I were inspired. "I'm to go back in an hour, after tea." *Pray let the bulge go unnoticed.*

No one blinked an eye except at Miss Hollow's exasperated tromping up the stairs.

"Now, there's a woman needs a man like a cake needs frosting," said Bates.

"You hush your sass," said Mrs. Wiggins, but we knew she felt the same way.

"Mary could make the baby stop, couldn't you, Mary?" said Bates.

"Aye, but I'm in scullery, aren't I?"

I set to peeling potatoes and rinsing them, and slicing the bread, and cleaning anything Cook put her hand on almost before it were put down, so as to keep ahead and take my time after.

I scrubbed up and quick dabbed on a bit of Miss Lucilla's rose scent when I were collecting her tea tray.

"What's that pong?" said Nut, waving his hand back and forth over his nose.

"You'll want to be washing that grubby wee paw," I said to him, "before Bates cuts it off to use for a blacking cloth."

"He wouldn't," said Nut, tucking his fingers into his vest pockets and stepping back.

"He might."

But Nut were done sniffing me. Thanks to my brothers, I'd learned long ago with little boys that distraction saves the day more often than not.

Mrs. Wiggins and Eliza were indignant that I'd be traipsing out in such a mess of weather—and wouldn't they have whinged if they'd known where I were headed? But out I went into the drizzle and grime of that November evening, to find the boy I were longing for with all my skin and spirit. There were indeed a dread fog that evening. It didn't matter a bird splash that I'd prettied my hair, as it were wet and dangling in two minutes out of doors.

This leads to that. There were plenty before that almighty kiss and Lord knows plenty after, so where did the leading *start*? One thing is clear: it were the fog, that particular night, that led to the kiss, wrapping us around in mystery, so even the plainest thing—a girl, and a boy in uniform—even that were given portent. And that kiss led straight to where you are and to where I be now.

I had only the time it would otherwise take to get to

Messrs. Finley & Dobbs, Apothecary, which were perhaps
eighteen minutes, there and back. I paused at the end of
Neville Street, dithering, wondering should I keep going
over to Russell Square and what were the chances he'd
even show his face?

My name were called, "Mary!" bringing to mind an
owl that haunted the lane back in Pinchbeck. But it weren't
an owl, not in London. It were him, Caden Tucker. Liar,
scoundrel, and heart's delight, though only the third did I
have a hint of yet.

"Out for a stroll?" he said.

"Not likely," I said. "When the air's as woolly as a
sheep's behind."

"Oh, then it's me you're looking for," he said, with
those eyes as bright as first daylight in the gray mist.

He caught me up with both his hands at my waist. My
heart jumped and my hands landed on his damp jacket
shoulders. The fog were so close that even as our bodies
bumped together his face were not entirely real until his
mouth were on mine. I closed my eyes and tasted him,
hungry as I'd never been.

Eliza had told me, the day we met this boy, how kissing
him might be. She'd listed the color of his eyes and the
shape of his lips and the slight beard that softened his jaw
and had never yet felt a blade—teasing me to consider
what I'd forfeited by not pouncing on him as she claimed
she would have if she hadn't promised herself to Bates.

But all his fine features that she'd mooned about—none of that were visible as I were *chewing* on him like it were my one chance to escape starvation, and he were clasping me like I were the thing he needed most in the world.

"Oi!" An angry gent appeared out of the mist and collided with us. His cane, and luck, saved him from a nasty tumble.

We were tossed apart, me dizzy with doing what I'd never have done if the day had been a fine one.

"What's the time?" I gasped. But Caden Tucker had melted into the gray, with the briefest salute and a grin on his face as if he'd won a prize for all of England.

OLIVER 1888

Father

"Mr. Chester," asked the boy one day, while sweeping the classroom floor, "do you think Frederick looks like the Prince of Wales?"

"Why do you ask that?"

"He thinks he might be the bastard son of the Prince of Wales. That's what he says."

"It is . . . possible, Nelligan, that the Prince of Wales does indeed have . . . a son . . . or more than one bastard son. But I think I can guarantee that Frederick Mills is not one of them."

"Because he doesn't look the same?"

"That would be a good place to start." Oliver lifted the dustpan from its nail by the door and crouched to hold it in place for James to sweep in the debris.

Oliver had had his own dream, when he was about James's age. It wasn't the Prince of Wales he'd yearned for, but the author Charles Dickens, who'd frequently come visiting, to hear the music on Sundays in the chapel. Oliver had convinced himself, briefly, that the great man came to see *him*, Oliver Chester, secretly loving him so much that he'd used the name for his famous character the orphan Oliver Twist.

"Who do you think I might look like?" asked James.

Oliver considered.

"I mean, if I don't ever . . . meet . . . my father, isn't it funny that I might still look like him?"

"Yes," said Oliver. This was the sort of conversation that made him want to hide in a cupboard.

"Or my mother?" said James. "My real mother?"

"You likely resemble both of them," said Oliver.

"But I'll never know, will I?"

"Nor will any of us," said Oliver. "Which of my parents needed spectacles, I wonder. Who gave me these ears, or the eyebrows of which I'm very proud?"

That seemed to brighten the boy up.

"It's like what you were saying in the lesson, isn't it, sir? About Henry the Eighth and his fiery-tempered daughter, Queen Elizabeth. About inherited traits? Only we *have* the traits and we'll never know if they're inherited, or something we invented for our own selves."

The boy had a point.

"You'd better assume it's all up to you," said Oliver. "And be content with looking like yourself, as there's no one else for comparison."

JAMES 1888

Now a Big Chap

What he saw Outside was real, James knew that, but not *real* real. It might be brighter, louder, sharper, than any dull day in the hospital, but there were a locked gate and a high wall keeping it out of reach. He could happily spy but luckily not have to go out there. The little plays that unfolded beneath his branch were almost imaginings—like the history stories that Mr. Chester told them during lessons, and even James's memories of Mama Peevey and the shop. All that had really happened, but long, long ago.

Voices floated directly upward, so James listened to plenty from the Outside that never went on in his own world. Along with the hawkers' cries, he heard cursing from soldiers and drunken bets and lovey-dovery between young men and their ladies.

"What *is* this place?" one girl asked her beau after they'd been pressing up against the high wall, so stuck together that James couldn't quite see what they were doing through the foggy dusk.

"It's an asylum," said the man. "Loonies and demented children."

"Ahh!" she cried. "What are we doing *here*?" She dragged him off while James wished it were a chestnut tree so's he'd have conkers to pelt them with. That gave him the idea to take pebbles next time, to have ammunition at the ready.

A band of tidy children came along one time, clustered around a nursemaid pushing a perambulator. Rich, thought James. They had pillows full of feathers, probably, a football for each boy, sweets every day. One of the boys was whining for an ice cream.

"You hush now," the nursemaid said. "Your papa doesn't permit whining. He'll give you away and you'll end up in *there*." She jerked her chin toward the wall, toward the very branch that James was gripping. "They eat *mice* in there, for a special treat! Do you hear me, Alexander? There's no such thing as ice cream for an orphan. . . ."

James sent a pebble straight off, and pinged the brim of her hat. Alexander got such a scolding that James laughed out loud with no one noticing. What was an ice cream, anyway? It sounded divine.

The bell rang. James shinnied down the tree and tore

across the yard. It was a Departure Day, with a ceremony to watch and an orange for every foundling. Walter didn't like oranges because his fingers got sticky, so if James was a chum, he might have two oranges before nightfall. And it wasn't just any old senior boys leaving; this group included Harvey Hooper and Monty Forbes, as well as the one and only Lionel "Tubbs" Tubman. This was James's lucky day! Harvey was off to be a sailor. Monty, who had somehow learned to play the trumpet, was joining the British Army as a band boy. Tubbs—James didn't even mind switching to his Sunday collar to celebrate—Tubbs would be a butcher's boy in the Fulham Road.

"They've all got good placements," Frederick told James. "The Foundling Hospital finds somewhere for everyone. Maybe I'll be a banker, if my mother doesn't come back to collect me. Or a—"

"But who would hire Tubbs to play with knives?" said James. "The newsboys will be shouting about human blood in the sawdust before you know it."

They slid into the chapel gallery. Usually it was Mr. Byrd who spoke on Departure Days, with his lame sister, Miss Byrd, sitting in the front row to hear the music. She'd never got married, because of her leg, so she came alone. But her brother's words of uplift and guidance were so boring that she often fell dead asleep. The boys made bets on just when her chin would drop to her chest.

Today, however, there was a guest speaker. Dr. Joshua Merkin had once been a foundling. Not at the same time with Mr. Chester. He was older than Mr. Chester by about a foot's worth of whiskers. But now he was a physician who had attended the Lord Mayor of London. He carried a heavy gold watch and had six horses to pull his carriage. He knew what happened inside a human body, how to fix a broken arm or what to do when the liver misbehaved. He told his audience about the doctors over a hundred years ago, who had attended the earliest foundlings, how they had been great scientists, made great medical discoveries, and been great teachers to those who followed. Dr. Merkin seemed very proud of himself and rubbed his round belly more than once, setting off giggles amongst the girls on the other side of the chapel. He shook the departing foundlings by the hand, even the young women, reminding them to be ever grateful and wishing them wisdom in their choice of employ.

James, suddenly a Big Chap with the departure of this crew, began to consider what might be waiting Outside for him.

MARY 1877

Telling About Love

It were near unbearable to wait all those minutes till another Thursday come along, but by then there were no need of fog to prompt us. Meeting to meeting those next weeks, I scarce could bite a pie or drink my tea or rub clean my teeth, nor tell a story to Nut or blow out the candle, but I were thinking what else I wished my mouth were doing instead.

The time came, we did not stop with kisses. I were as eager as he, I will not deny it. There hadn't been a boy before who liked me, not for teasing and flirting or kissing or any of the rest of it. I'd not had anyone to say I were pretty or to bundle me round in his ready arms as if I were a true delight to hold on to. I couldn't think, aside from Eliza's backside touching me in bed, that anyone more than a child had touched me at all since Mam had died.

All along I knew it weren't ladylike, but a lady were never what I got up in the morning to be.

Enough to say that the kissing were hot and even frantic. Our layers of clothing were an obstacle that had us laughing while we tugged to disarrange things. My hands rushed all over him, touching places they had *never* touched before. He were heated and bucking, saying the wildest things, calling me sweetheart and slipping his fingers above my stockings, fumbling with my drawers until I tore them down for him, we were that warm. Funny how even though it were new, we both had the idea of what to do next.

I were eager, like I said. When he pushed into me, I cried out, ready—aching—for pleasure and not expecting it to hurt that way.

"Oh no!" he gasped. "I didn't realize—"

"Go on!" I cried. He kissed me for one soft moment before we galloped on in the most fevered romp . . . this was where a kiss could lead? It took a person over, body humming and spirit noisy in song.

That were Caden and me, that afternoon near dark in the furthest corner of the burial ground at St. Andrew's Gardens, on the grave of EVERETT MULDOWER 1749–1806 and HIS WIFE, ADA, who lived another twenty-six years without him.

After, we barely spoke, for giggling and brushing off and snatching extra kisses, until we looked about and saw that it were truly night. If I did not run full-speed, the

Allyns' tea would include bread sliced by Nut and sprinkled over with fingertips.

So run I did.

"You're as pink-cheeked as St. Nicholas," said Eliza.

"I've been running," I told her. "I were distracted by
the sights and got late. My under-bodice is pinching."

"Red face, guilty conscience?" she asked, pricking me
with those dark eyes.

"Ha, ha," I managed.

"And what do you know? You weren't the only one out
there prowling in the dark," she said, nodding toward the
door as Bates banged it open.

"Well, well, well," she said to him. "Another stray, coming in for shelter." Her voice were tight and peculiar, but
Bates gave her bum a pat and she cheered up some. I took
the moment to repin my hair, feeling Caden's hands in it,
tugging while he whispered, "So pretty, so soft . . ."

After that first time, Caden and I wasted few moments
on chatter. We were always laughing, but we were past
flirtation, always in a hurry, always fiddling with clothing
in the way. We never did chance being naked, pressed together all the way from lips to toes. Nor did we take the
time again to go so far as the cemetery. I never saw his
bare back, nor his shoulders, though I could feel them well
enough, as I slid my hands up under his shirt, putting my
palms flat against the warm wide strength of him.

We were most often in the dairy shed, behind the
Allyn house, where no one went after the day's milk were

fetched each morning. It were chilly in there, being made of hunking great stones; another reason not to dally about without covering.

We thought, once, of going to his own bed, in the little place off the barracks stable where he had a cot, but it were raining that night, too far to walk in the wet, with me having to come back and look presentable at the end of it. So we stuck with the nearby and I were rosy-faced but dry when next seen by Mrs. Wiggins.

What possessed me? I'd been a girl with common sense up till then. All the days between our minutes together, sense never won. Not over . . . over the *lust* of it. Whatever were I thinking?

Nothing clever, it's clear now. Clear as the first cry on a winter morning. "Pies, ladies! Fresh pies!" Only it were "Lies, ladies! All lies!"

JAMES 1888

Guildford Street

An old pieman stood himself on the very same cobble every day, his basket so heavy to start with that it sat by his feet— or *on* his feet when the mud was bad. When the breeze was right, the smell of meat floated up to James in the tree, making his stomach grumble even if he'd just had his dinner. This old man's cap looked like one of his own pies, with his hair sticking out in tufts from under it. The customers called him Pie Peter, and he'd sing two hundred times in an afternoon: "Savory pies! Fresh and tasty, buy them hasty! Pies! Savory pies! Fresh and tasty, buy them hasty! Pies!"

Late on a drizzly day, James spied a gang of boys creeping up on Pie Peter. Their clothes were tattered, enormous, maybe parts of men's suits, torn off to make the lengths right or tied on with string. Some of their feet were bare, some were wrapped in newspapers or rags; some wore shoes of a sort, but none with laces and none with hose. James was tempted to peel off his own stockings and toss them down, just to see if the urchins would know what to use them for.

The two in front were playacting: the littlest boy began crying at a nod from his partner. He belched out such a boohooing that he drowned out "Savory pies!"

The old man leaned over to him, maybe tender or maybe just to shut his noise, but those other scamps scooted in from behind and snatched pies right out of the basket! Pie Peter hollered and swung his cap as if it were a stick that could strike the villains down.

James laughed so hard he nearly slipped off the branch. He climbed down, still hearing the small boy's shout, "We was hungry 'n' you gots pies!"

James lay in his bed that night, surrounded by the familiar night sounds: Walter wheezing, Frederick snoring in squeaky huffs, Adam Bernard whimpering as always, as if he were dreaming about greedy rats crawling over his mattress, Michael Angelo grinding his teeth like he'd got the hardest of boiled sweets between his molars.

James propped himself up on an elbow, looking around in the dark until it didn't seem quite so black.

"Hey!" he whispered at Frederick's cot. "You awake?"

"Shht!" shushed someone, but it was a boy hiss, not a matron hiss.

Frederick rolled over. "What?" he grumbled.

"I've got an idea," said James.

"Save it for morning."

"It's about food," said James. "Aren't you hungry?"

James could feel Frederick sitting up. He glanced toward the west end of the dormitory, thirty cots away, where the matron had a tiny room. There was no light.

"She's on rounds," whispered James. "Old Aldercott."

"Full-of-Snot," mumbled Frederick.

"Come on." James slid off the bed. His nerve was up; he had to stop himself from running across the floor. Frederick would surely follow. He tiptoed away from Matron's closet to the east stairwell. A scuffling behind him, a grunt and curse. Not just Frederick but Walter, too, Frederick trying to stop him. James snapped his fingers, then swiped one finger across his throat. At the top of the stairs, James pressed them both against the wall.

"There's no messing things up," he whispered. "Quit yapping or go back to bed."

Nods from both plus a salute from Walter.

The kitchens were locked. Of course they would be, in the middle of the night.

"All this way for nothing," Frederick complained. "You think you're so clever."

James would prove how clever.

"We aren't here for the kitchen," he said. "That's next time. Follow me."

The masters had a separate dining room, not so fancy as the one where the governors gathered, and not so plain as the boys' refectory. There must be something in there worth having? James crept along next to the wall,

Frederick and Walter bumbling behind him. His team needed training if they were to match the Pie Peter raiders.

Ahh, the door handle clicked neatly open and his chilled feet stepped onto a carpet.

"Cor," said Frederick.

"Shhh."

Moonlight shone faintly through the window, striping the table in the middle of the room and illuminating a silver tray on a lace cloth. There sat a sugar bowl, a pitcher for cream, and—oh glory!—a jam pot with a spoon poking up through the hole in its lid.

James reached across the table to pull the cloth toward them. Frederick lunged for the sugar bowl, but James smacked his arm away.

"Ow!"

"We're not pirates," said James. "We'll take turns."

"Who says?"

"I say." James had a hand on each precious vessel, one covering the sugar, the other holding the jam pot. "You obey the rules, Frederick, or you won't come next time."

"Who says?"

"I say." James handed the bowl to Walter, who pinched up sugar between thumb and fingers and drizzled it onto his tongue with a sigh of rapture. James flipped off the jam pot lid to find marmalade! He scooped a spoonful into his mouth. *Ah!* The slightly bitter burst of orange seemed as bright as sunshine for the moment that it lasted. Walter passed the sugar bowl to Frederick. James handed the jam pot and spoon to Walter. On the next trade, James could hardly taste the sprinkle of sugar over the lively bitter sweetness of the marmalade. Frederick must have found the same thing because at his turn he tipped the bowl and poured a stream of sugar into his open mouth.

"Hey!" cried Walter.

"Pig!" cursed James, joggling Frederick's arm. Sugar sprayed across the table and floor, but Frederick wouldn't let go of the bowl.

"What did you go and do that for?" Frederick glared at them. "You spilled it, stupid!"

Walter was already pressing moist palms against the snowfall on the tabletop, licking them off and pressing again, picking up every last speck.

"You forfeit marmalade," said James. "For being a pig with the sugar."

"Nasty stuff, anyway." Frederick retreated to a corner and quietly finished off the whole bowl of sugar by himself. James and Walter passed the spoon back and forth until the jam pot was empty.

Sneaking back up, Walter murmured, "This was the best night of my life, ever."

"Since we came here," said James.

He spent all of prayers next morning thinking about how that marmalade had tasted on his tongue, from the first lick to the very last sliver of orange nibbled off his lips. It was hard to think of Jesus Christ under such circumstances, He who likely never had jam in all His life.

Telling About Christmas

I woke up blinking dizzy, with some quick and wily rodent darting about my belly. It brought my innards rushing to my mouth as I sat up. *Ohh,* I didn't like that, not one bit. No time to pull on shoes, my bare feet stumbled me down four flights, lickety-split, across the yard to the servants' privy.

Eliza were waiting when I came back up, eyeing me like a market fish she weren't likely to put in her basket.

"What got you moving so fast this morning?"

"Not well," I mumbled, sloshing water from the jug over my wrists. But then, with the knot of doom tightening itself around my throat, I produced a sunny smile.

"All better now!"

And weren't I then as strong and fast as two? The way I collected the boots for polishing, and hustled room to

room, sweeping the grates, carting down the ashes, light-
ing the fires . . . like I were ablaze myself.

I wasted no time a-trying to trick myself. I knew full
well that I were knapped and having a baby. My life were
over at the same instant it had just begun. Every bit of me
trembled; in love, in a panic to keep it hid, and sure too
that I would die the way Mam had, birthing Nan. And
what would I do, anyway, without Mam? That was what
set me to whimpering, pretending it were a cinder in my
eye, not all the other terrible true things that occurred to
me in those few minutes, but only not having me mam to
tell—or not tell, however I might choose.

I scuttled to the cellar with the ash bucket to finish
choking and sniffling. Lordy, I were sick of crying. I sat
there still as stone for a bit, the cold air clearing the heat
and damp from my face, soothing me even.

Finally I thought of Caden and got a blow of hope
through me, like when you think there's only gray ash in
the grate, but with a few strong puffs you've got sparks like
scarlet dust and then, wouldn't you know it? Day after day,
the fire lights up after all, from one tiny, fiery ember straight
to having enough water hot for Lady's bath, and the tea,
and the washing up, and oh, if it's Monday, the laundry.

So I kept Caden's cheeky smile right there in my mind,
to get me back up the stairs and doing what had to be
done to pass the hours—how many would it be?—days,
maybe . . . until I'd touch that smile with my own chapped
fingers.

OLIVER 1888

Kings

The boy could rattle off the kings and queens of England right from the beginning, from Egbert in 828 AD, long before William the Conqueror, right up to Queen Victoria, including the dates of all their reigns. He was keen, all right. Oliver liked to think of tasks for him. Little mental challenges. It wasn't right to favor him, Oliver knew that, but what was a teacher to do with a bright boy? He was naturally inclined to lists, so let him proceed. . . .

"Mr. Chester, I've learned what you suggested. Shall I tell you the kings whose names began with the letter E?"

"If you can recite while you clean the slates, boy, I'll listen."

James cheerfully dipped a cloth into the bucket of murky water and began. "Egbert, Ethelwulf, Ethelbald, Ethelbert, Ethelred. All those Ethels were Ethelwulf's sons, and so was Alfred, who came next, but he's not an *E*. Then Edward the Elder, Ethelstan, Edmund the Magnificent, Eadred, Eadwig the All-Fair—"

"Watch it, Nelligan, you're splashing the floor. How many are there, anyway?"

"Edgar the Peaceable, Edward the Martyr . . . I think there are twenty, sir, but does Elizabeth count? She'd make it twenty-one."

"And why wouldn't she count?"

"She's not a king, sir, is she?"

"Then you'll have to rename your category if you want to include her."

"All right then, *monarchs* whose names—"

"Hey, I asked for clean slates, not lakes, boy!"

"I'll mop the floor after, sir. Sir?"

"Yes, Nelligan."

"We both have brown hair, don't we? And we both think gruel is foul."

"Indeed we do."

"We both like knowing things about kings."

"You've got quite a list!"

"And football! We both love football!"

"Better than anything."

"Don't you think that's a lot of things the same?" James wrung out the cloth and spread it neatly on the edge of the bucket before looking straight into Oliver's eyes. "What if you're my father?"

Oliver caught his breath. "Oh, my dear boy . . . I'm afraid that's not possible . . . I . . . I'm nobody's father." It pinched him to say it. "And nobody's son."

MARY 1878

Telling About Telling

Telling Caden one simple sentence were an act of fierce bravery, and took some working up to. *No rush,* I'd say to myself . . . *I've got time before there'll be anything to notice. Aside from feeling wobbly in the mornings, and I can do better at hiding that.* But on smarter days, time ticked like a grandfather clock between my ears, the pendulum banging away like a drum.

The worst were seeing him, my mouth and body with all the same yearnings, but thinking, *Lordy, no!* and then thinking, *Well, the horse is long gone from this barn so why not?* But then thinking it were not fair to go on without him knowing the truth, and should I not tell him? Such worry, of course, about whatever he'd say, imagining every scene; him being sick into the gutter, him giving me a slap, him bestowing a twist of peppermints with a promise inside . . .

The day came when I swore to myself not to dally any further. *Spit it out, girl, and take whatever comes.* Hard to remember, with all that passed later, that I were clutching the irregular notion there were some romance in it.

"I've something to tell you," I said, without even a hello. He patted the bench and I shivered a little, sitting down next to him, waiting for the familiar feel of his arm slid around my shoulders, and him tucking the top of my head under his chin.

"Face as grave as a tombstone," he laughed, doing just what I'd imagined, grinding his chin into my scalp, making me squirm.

"Stop!" I said, but laughing too, letting another minute slip by, letting him kiss me, letting my heart skip one more time . . . *Is this the last kiss before he knows? Is this? Will he shout, curse me, cry, run? Will he grin like a daddy?*

"Well, what is it, then?" he said. "What's your urgent matter?"

Not knowing what I'd see in those blue blinkers at the end of my next sentence, I looked away.

"I'm . . . I . . . I'll be having a baby."

His arm twitched as he sat up straight. He were deadly quiet.

I said, "You're not going to faint, are you?"

He stood, and sat, and stood again.

"Mary." He knelt in front of me, his hands taking mine. "I'm . . . I don't know what to say. You . . . Oh Lord . . . a baby?" He stood up again, like there were a moth in his britches. Me sitting still all the while, watching.

"I'm . . . surprised, but I suppose I shouldn't be," he said. "It's . . . Are you certain?"

I nodded. He sat. He closed his eyes. He opened them. He took my hand and bounced it ever so slightly.

"Don't girls know about these things? What to do at such a time?"

I pulled my hand away.

His eyes implored me, like a beggar's eyes watching a market basket, wanting something there were no chance he'd get. My mouth were suddenly as dry as yesterday's cake.

He ducked his head and laid it in my lap, where I could not resist stroking his dark hair.

"I don't know yet." I answered what he hadn't asked. "I've not worked things out. I wanted . . . I thought I should . . . hear what you might say."

"Oh, Mary"—sitting up again—"it's a big, big thing you're telling me! You can't be surprised that I'm . . . I'm shocked a little. But I'll come round to it, I'm sure I will. If only, can I go away to think about it? Can we meet tomorrow?"

Well, I'd had weeks to get used to the idea and he were just hearing. Of course there were some dazement on his part. It weren't till after we said goodbye—with a bit of a cuddle included—that I were struck with the notion that I might not see him again.

The Bloody Nose

Oliver gazed at the second-form boys studiously writing out the Act of Succession, 1534. When Henry VIII married Anne Boleyn and their daughter, Elizabeth, was born, the king had declared his first child, Mary, a bastard and no longer heir to the throne. He changed his mind, of course, more than once, but Oliver often wondered how the whim of one man in heat had affected the condition of bastards and foundlings throughout British history. Why was it only the king's own state of wedlock that determined whether it mattered, for the rest of time, that anyone else was married—or not—when a child was born?

"Mr. Chester?"

Oliver looked at James Nelligan.

"Permission to speak, sir?"

"Yes, Nelligan."

"It's Walter, sir." James pointed. Walter was hunched over with his hands pressed to his face.

Oliver stood up. "What's the mat—?"

Blood was bubbling out from between the boy's fingers.

Oh dear, not blood. Oliver sat down, instantly light-headed. "Run and get one of the nurses, would you?" he mumbled. James sped toward the door, as Oliver pulled a thankfully fresh handkerchief out of his pocket.

"Give him this," he said, handing it to the boy named Aiken. "And tell him to press the nose closed." The children clustered around Walter, shielding him from sight, but making wildly appreciative noises that told Oliver the flow was so far undiminished. He went to the door and saw James trotting beside a young, hurrying nurse, apparently demonstrating the bleeding volcano.

"Hello," said the nurse. She looked quite jangled.

Oliver tipped his head and then clapped his hands. "Please allow the nurse to come through. Collect your copybooks—calmly, please—from your desks and file into the hallway. Give Mr. Raleigh some breathing room." He felt better at once, away from the splashes of blood on the floor.

Walter Raleigh's got a bleeding nose, he thought. He still got a bit of a chuckle when a famous name showed up in odd moments as entirely incongruous with the life of a schoolboy.

"Raleigh's bad luck is your good," Oliver announced. "I

hereby— Hold on! You will complete your copy of the first Act of Succession before tomorrow's lesson and give some consideration to what the Second and Third Acts may have contained. Until then you are dismissed."

That set off a whoop and a general stampede.

"Oh! Except—" Oliver grabbed the nearest arm. "Aiken. Aiken, you wait for Raleigh. Accompany him back to the ward, would you please, when he's ready?"

When the nurse was done pinching the nose and mopping the face, Oliver sent the boys off, Aiken's arm generously slung about Raleigh's waist for support.

"Thank you," said Oliver to the nurse. "I'm not so bold with blood and mess like that."

She laughed. "Most men aren't, for all their playing at war."

"I haven't seen you before," said Oliver, stacking books neatly under his arm. "Are you recently arrived?"

"Yes," she said.

He locked the classroom and they walked together along the corridor.

"Where did you work before this?"

"At the Lying-In Hospital, on Old Street. I started there as a cleaner when . . . when I were just a girl. As time went on, I helped with the babies and learned more about nursing. It were a marvel, so many babies being born. All the uproar! Never a dull moment, I tell you."

"Why did you decide to come here?"

It seemed to Oliver that her hesitation was as lively as a match being struck.

"I . . . I . . . The babies there, they all have mothers," she said. "The mothers . . . they all are . . . married. It seemed that here . . . there would be more *need*. . . ."

"I understand," he said, quietly. Even as an adult, he prickled with the shame he'd been taught to carry. But it seemed this stranger might understand what he usually pretended wasn't so. "I was a foundling," he heard himself whisper. "I know how these boys feel."

The bright flush of interest on her face surprised and warmed him, though all she said was "Ah!"

She was awfully pretty, Oliver thought. Soft-looking hair.

A moment later, she spoke again. "That boy."

"Walter Raleigh? With the nosebleed? He—"

"No, no. The other one, who came to find me."

"James Nelligan," said Oliver.

"James? That's his name? With the very blue eyes?"

"Yes. He's a clever boy, one of my best."

"He . . . seemed, yes, clever. And he cared about his friend. That's *nice*," she said, as if the word weren't quite what she intended.

"They raise them up here for a purpose, you know," said Oliver. "I'm an unusual case, staying close to home. So to speak. Most of them go off to be soldiers or bakers' boys or . . . well, if Walter Raleigh is permitted to pick up pins for a tailor, he should consider himself lucky. But with James, I expect he could be a teacher, or better."

"Really?"

"Oh, yes indeed. Out there"—he nodded vaguely to

encompass the wide world beyond the walls—"who knows how far he might go? But, of course, as a foundling . . . we're taught to be grateful, you understand? Grateful just to be alive. Pasts and futures are equally cloudy."

· JAMES 1888

What Changed Things

Walter rushed into the dormitory on a Sunday afternoon. The boys had two hours all of their own on Sundays after chapel, so James was lying on his bed, particularly *not* reading the Bible.

Walter always panted slightly, like the Peeveys' old dog Toby, waiting under the table for a lump of gristle.

"I have to tell you . . ." Huffing.

"What?" James rubbed the lump in his cuff out of habit, checking on the lemon drop that he carried around with him. Thanks to the ladies at Sunday dinner, he was ready to pay for anything he needed. Walter saw, and got notions straightaway.

"What'll you give me?"

"What could you know that I don't?" said James.

"There're girls arriving today."

"Well, I know that. I've got a window, haven't I?"

"From Kent," Walter said. "From Homefield."

Ah. *That* was news to James. He eased the sweet out from the hem of his sleeve and handed it over, not too fuzzy. Walter popped it straight in, smirking, never a boy to keep money in the bank.

"What are you going to do?" Walter said. "Wait! Wait for me!"

But James was already in the corridor, not wanting Walter to follow. Alone, he'd be better at sneaking. It was best—but also risky—to watch Reception Day from the main stairs. They didn't like bigger boys scaring the new-comers, so there were rules to keep them out of the way. But the officers and the matrons were busy and distracted, so James was soon stationed behind the railing, watching, wondering how he'd know Rose. It was four years since he'd seen her baby face screwed up and wailing. He'd jounced away down the road in that old cart, Mama Peevey's arm trying to keep James's little self from bouncing right off the seat, James looking back till there was nothing to see but dust.

James didn't need to know Rose, for there was Mama in the doorway. She . . . she seemed . . . shorter, rounder, to James, but as big as a dream. He jumped to his feet, her name falling out of his mouth without thinking.

"Mama!"

She twisted her head around, peering, eyes maybe straining after stepping in from the day to the shadows of the grand entrance. She was wearing the same Sunday dress he knew, gray with a blue stripe. It *was* Sunday, after all, but a Sunday dress from Homefield seemed olden, faded, in London.

All this in a tenth of a moment, seeing Mama stare around, awkward. Her confusion made James remember how this place had looked to him all that time ago: as posh and foreign as Buckingham Palace. And there was Rose, hidden behind Mama's skirt.

"Mama!" called James again. "Rose!" He flew down the stairs.

"Jamie!" Mama Peevey let go Rose's hand and moved toward him. James was swallowed, caught up in her dear, familiar arms. He had long ago darned up that place where tears might come from, as neatly as the toe of a sock. But Mama's hug tore all his knots apart, and he was gushing hard.

"That's enough now." It was Mr. Byrd growling, the rotten, meddling chaplain, usually called the Turd amongst the boys. "There'll be none of this here today. You, boy! Nelligan, is it?"

Mama let go of James. She looked at Byrd and fetched up Rose's hand again.

"You're not to be here, not at all." Byrd's hand clamped James's shoulder, pulling him back from Mama, just as Rose thought to hold on.

"James?" cried Rose. James would wager five lollipops she'd been hearing his name all her life, *James* this and *James* that: *You'll be with James when you go to London. There'll be big brother James to look out for you, lovey, nothing to worry about. When you go to live with James at the Foundling, Rosie . . .*

And here he was—the real thing. The real James, being yanked away before she'd even said hello-and-how-do-you-do. Mama was protesting, "Excuse me, sir, that's my boy, Jamie. . . ."

"Not anymore, madam," Mr. Byrd said. "He's one of ours now and he's in the wrong place. It is precisely this sort of scene that we try to avoid, you understand. Think of the upset. Think of the little girl."

A circle of newcomers had arrived while James wasn't noticing: terrified foundlings, and frowning foster parents.

Pushed along by Mr. Byrd toward one of the office doors, James suddenly stopped, wishing he could dig in his heels, imagining that the marble floor was a muddy rut outside the Peeveys' front door. The hand on his shoulder became heavier, pushier.

"I only want to see my mother," said James. "How can it hurt to see my mother? I haven't seen her in four years!"

"We have rules, Nelligan, and you have broken the rules."

"James!" Rose's shriek was newly urgent. Mama leaned on her awkwardly, then staggered to one side and slumped to the ground. Other foster parents hurried over, crowded around, hiding her from James.

At once, he had sparks in his fists. He pounded at Mr. Byrd's waistcoat, ducking at the same time, trying to sneak under grabbing hands. Mr. Byrd caught James's wrists and wrenched them with a furious twist. He leered into James's face, puffing with hot and oniony anger.

"You have just qualified for a room to yourself." His grip bit into James's neck, not allowing another glimpse of Mama or Rose. James was yanked, stumbling, down back stairs to a door that he had never seen. Mr. Byrd flung it open, flung James through it, and flung it shut again. With the click of a lock, James was alone and in such darkness as would make an owl entirely content.

ELIZA 1878

Follows Mary

There was no question that Mary was sneaking off somewhere more often than Thursday half days. One afternoon,
Eliza tied on her crossover shawl and dashed out on Mary's
tail, only to fall over a secret she hadn't come close to
guessing at.

You could have knocked Eliza over with a dustcloth,
she was that gobsmacked to see Mary meet up with Mr.
Tucker and another fellow, in Maiden Lane. She was a
canny one, that Mary! She'd kept it hid from Eliza, and
from Bates—oh! Wouldn't Bates be peeved! Eliza laughed
out loud right there. Ha! Here was the best kind of proof
that Mary wasn't the girl for Bates. She had more than one
pot on the boil, and Eliza hadn't been fooled for one
minute, had she? How the devil did Mary get herself met

up with Mr. Tucker? And weren't they all polite, bowing and nodding back and forth? It clearly hadn't progressed past how-de-dos, but things were like to move quickly where Mary was concerned, Eliza would be the first to say.

She didn't linger but raced back to Neville Street— skipping, almost, tickled! And wondering what pudding there'd be for tea.

MARY 1878

Telling About a Shift in the Wind

Lordy, I'd been girding against him not showing his face but there he were. Never did a heart dance as mine did right then.

"Caden!"

"Hello there," he said.

I could have flung my whole self at him, but his voice alarmed me, being something I had not heard before, and that were standoffish. I saw there were another chap beside him with a look on his face of watching me close.

"This is Jacob Vickers," said Caden. "Jacob, I'd like to introduce Miss Mary Finn."

Miss? Mr. Vickers bowed slightly.

"Hello." I nodded, polite but peeved. "Are you new

with the company?" Not giving a rat's tooth, just wanting my boy to myself.

"Hey," I whispered to Caden. "Can we have a minute alone? I've only got that much. I'm meant to be buying thread for Miss Hollow."

Caden glanced at Mr. Vickers. Mr. Vickers looked away and whistled no song at all but a noise like an old drawer.

"Go to the pie wagon at the corner," Caden told me. "I'll meet you there in five minutes."

I fretted at the corner, watching for Caden, wondering should I find a shop to buy the thread or wait? What if I missed him?

"Pins!" I heard the cry. "Needles and pins!"

There were a peddler girl right there, with all manner of ribbons and laces, buttons and threads. I bought what Miss Hollow wanted, so that were done. I wished I had a penny of my own, to buy a pretty.

At last I saw his cap with the bright blue band, hurrying through the hundred, nay, thousand other caps that bobbed along the street that morning. How did this funny, lovely boy become mine, out of all the boys in London?

"Only one minute," he said, panting and flushed.

"Time for a kiss?" I said, trying for saucy.

"Always that." He swooped in and kissed me, the barest, quickest, softest kiss, which I now know to have been his last.

"Have you kept our secret?" I asked him, linking my arm through his.

"Didn't I promise you?" he said.

We took a turn about the square.

"Did you think about me?"

"How could I not?" His chin lowered. "Mary." He looked down, looked up, touched my hair. "You don't . . . I need to know . . . you're not *angry*?"

"Angry?"

"I've done to you what I should kill a man for doing to one of my sisters," he said, now looking away.

"You wouldn't kill anyone," I scoffed. "And what if your sister were as happy as I am and you went about punching him in the nose?"

That laugh cheered us both up.

"Look, there!" he said. "The pin girl. I want to buy you something, for . . . I should say, as a token. . . ."

"I just bought Miss Hollow's thread from her."

"It's good luck, then," he said. "Close your eyes and wait for me."

Of course I did, with the tunes of Covent Garden calling and singing around me. Then he were back, taking my hand.

"No, no, keep your eyes shut," he whispered. He held my palm open, placed something there, and curled my fingers around it.

"I'm going now," he said.

"Caden!" I stomped and opened my eyes. "It weren't enough!"

"No, no," he said. "Shut." He laughed. "Count to ten

before you look at your treasure. I'll see you Thursday next and we'll have all the time in the world. I've got to go back now or they'll put me against the wall and shoot me."

I shut my eyes. His lips brushed my knuckles. I counted seven before I looked for his cap amidst the crowd. He must have run, because there were no glimpse of him. Would he be teased by his mate for having a sweetheart so brazen as to come looking for him?

I unfurled my fist to see a bright silver button, edged with tiny pinprick dots that resembled the finest lace on the hem of a petticoat. I squeezed it tight with such a smile that the pin girl waved at me as if she knew she had been part of a lovers' afternoon.

JAMES 1888

In the Dark

James punched the *damned* door after Mr. Byrd had locked it, but it hurt and he knew hitting it was stupid. Doors do not open because you punch them.

What had happened to Mama? Was she ill? Had she died up there on the floor while he was being dragged away by the Turd? James blushed, hot with mad, knowing he was thinking bad words, but they were easy to think: *The big, stinking Turd*. How could he not let James see his mama?

James kicked the door, but that hurt too. And it didn't sound like the door, just gave a dull *pft*. It was a brick wall, cold to touch. He'd got turned around in the dark, tears fogging his eyes. He would *not* cry. Mama was sick, or something worse. He rubbed his eyes hard, needing to see better. Ah, there, the slightest line of light, like a single golden hair laid across the floor, showing the bottom of the door. He didn't remember a light burning, but there must be one in the corridor out there.

James reached for the door and then traced his way around the tiny, empty room with his fingertips. He couldn't quite touch both sides of the room at the same time, but nearly. He swayed from side to side with his fingers outstretched, pushing himself off one wall to meet the other. It must be a closet. He rocked harder, mustering enough momentum to greet the walls with flat palms, back and forth, back and forth, breath jagged, till finally he stopped.

"Mama," he whispered. Utter silence. He held his breath. The room was so small and dark and quiet he might have had his head in a sack.

Then, footsteps!

Telling How the Cat Came Out of the Bag

I were in the privy and I were puking, like every morning then. The door yanked open and Eliza caught me, not with my skirts up, as would have been shame enough, but with my head in the hole, letting loose my breakfast. Though I hadn't been up to much in the way of breakfast and that had been her clue.

"Aha!" she cried. "I knew it!"

I wiped my mouth and glared at her, wishing I'd brought a cup of water as I'd remembered to the day before.

She only smirked. "You're having his baby."

She said it as fact. The proof were in the rank smell lingering, making a lie utterly useless.

I nodded ever so slight, squeezing my eyes shut

against the truth. But there were some relief in hearing it spoken loud and clear like that, in having someone know. Eliza could help, maybe.

"You're a worse slut than ever I realized," she said.

"What?"

"You come along with your little angel face, blinking your big green eyes, meanwhile waggling your scrawny bum at every man in sight, never considering how other people have got plans of their own . . ." And she began to cry, as if me being knapped were somehow *her* heartache!

"What, Eliza? What are you saying?" It were more than confusing.

"It's not as if you love him!" She were weeping and furious, like a child mad for his share of pudding. "For you it's some kind of—of what? A game? *I'm* the one who loves him!"

Loves *who*?

With no warning, she slapped me, hard, her whole palm striking my whole cheek, *zang!* My head snapped under the speed of it and cracked against the doorframe. The thud echoed in my ear while I reeled against the wall. I groped for the hole and puked again, my face and poor noggin popping with pain. I stood up, hoping she'd gone, but she were still filling the doorway, with me a prisoner.

"I need to breathe or I'll swoon," I said. "Let me out." I tried to push past. "You've got it wrong."

Did she think I loved *Bates*?

She snatched at my apron to look under. I swatted her hand away. "I'll puke on you, Eliza, I swear. Let me out!"

She stepped back into the yard, me bursting out nearly on top of her in my rush to find air.

And praise be, Mrs. Wiggins stuck her nose out the kitchen with a scowl on her face hot enough to burn toast.

"I'll have your hides, the two of you, if you're not in this kitchen before my next breath."

Eliza started moving, and I flung my words at her back. "Eliza! You've got it wrong. It's not Bates, for Heaven's sake!"

She stopped dead in her tracks and spun around, me thunking right into her.

"Either you're a liar," she whispered at me, her face up so close I could see into her nose, "and you've got ideas about keeping Bates, or you're no better than a slut from the Sailor's Delight. You might as well have rouge all over your cheeks and a blouse cut down to show off your titties. Which aren't much worth showing, I'll tell you right now."

She clumped under Cook's arm holding the door, while I staggered after, feeling like I'd just been slapped again. Had Mrs. Wiggins heard us? A chill crackled up my spine. Even if she hadn't caught what Eliza had said out in the yard, she'd no doubt be hearing it all by dinnertime.

ELIZA 1878

Manages Not to Speak

With a roar fighting to burst from her lungs, Eliza managed to cross the kitchen, climb the stairs, and get herself to the nursery sink, where she poured icy water over her wrists and splashed her neck until her bodice and chemise were wet through. *Good, I didn't spit it all out to Cook,* she thought, *because I want to get this right.* Eliza wanted to taste every morsel of revenge and not waste a single drop through a silly fit of temper. She'd see the end of Mary Finn . . . and so would Bates.

JAMES 1888

Liberty

"Let me out!" he yelled. "Right now!"

A burble of words from outside, more than one voice.

"Where's my mother?"

The grinding sound of an old lock. James stepped back. What if Byrd-Turd had brought a strap or a cane? James's legs began to jiggle, waiting, hearing the key sticking. He still tingled to hit Mr. Byrd, but he cared more about seeing Mama. He'd better remember that. He huffed out his breath, ready to be quiet until he'd got what he wanted.

The door opened. It wasn't Mr. Byrd who'd come, it was Mr. Chester with that new nurse, holding a lantern. James didn't mean to whimper, but the noise slipped out, as if he hadn't been brave in there, facing midnight in a closet.

James sagged toward Mr. Chester, who propped him up and led him into the hallway. The nurse lifted her lamp, shining too bright into his eyes.

"I'm not crying," he said. "Mr. Chester, I'm *not*. But . . . but . . . I want to see my mama. She's here. She brought Rose, but something happened . . . I . . . She . . ."

Mr. Chester put a hand on his shoulder, warm, like a mitten.

"She had a little spell. The journey with Rose was a tiring one and she . . . Look, Nelligan, you won't be able to see her today. You're lucky we've been allowed to spring you from prison. Mr. Byrd sent me down, hoping you'd listen to sense."

James had promised himself to be quiet. Why was it harder with Mr. Chester than with the Turd?

"No!" *Stop it, eyes! No crying!*

The nurse crouched down so that her face was close to his. Her eyes were wet too.

"I have an idea." Her voice was soft, a little husky. "Mr. Byrd insists that you go up to the ward now and stay there. Nurse Aldercott is waiting for you. Mr. Byrd wants you to reflect, and to pray . . . for control of your temper. But your . . . your *mama*—" The nurse paused and stood up as though her legs might be stiff. She put a hand out to touch James's arm. "She's resting tonight. Mr. Byrd were kind enough to take her in. His sister is caring for her. If you show . . . *earnest* repentance, possibly Mr. Byrd will permit you to visit tomorrow, before your mama sets out on her journey home." The nurse looked up at Mr. Chester. "Do you think this might be agreeable?"

"It would seem our only course. Nelligan, I will talk to Mr. Byrd myself. Thank the nurse, and make yourself scarce."

"Yes, sir. Thank you, sir. Thank you, Nurse."

James stumbled up the steps, grabbing for the railing. His thoughts swarmed inside his head, buzzing and knocking into each other. Mama was sick. Rose was here, somewhere, having her hair chopped off and surely very frightened. Mr. Chester and the nurse might think that the chaplain would allow him to visit Mama Peevey, but it did not seem too likely to James. Why should he wait until tomorrow, only to be told no? Lucky that Nurse Aldercott was so old and nearly blind. He *would* pray—pray that no one saw him climb the tree and go over the wall.

MARY 1878

Telling About Time Like Treacle

Every hour, I expected to be hurled out in the street, but every hour passed, and then days, and I were still scrubbing or peeling or slicing or hauling, just as I'd been doing every day since I'd come here, as if there were no world outside the scullery and no story unfolding except in my own head. It were most unnerving. Mrs. Wiggins were snappy and Bates were scarce, making letter deliveries for His Lordship all over town. Eliza were oddly polite while ignoring me but making a big show in the attic of sleeping on the floor. I tried, of course, to say a few words, begging to clear things up, but she would leave the room if I started, and never answer.

Thursday came again. I were in such a state of bewilderment over wondering each minute if I'd be working or loony by the next minute, that I near forgot the day of the week.

"Are you not going out, Mary?" asked Cook. "I was going to ask if you'd bring me back a packet of that tea I like, with rose hips. I'd have asked Eliza, only you got it last time and you know the kind."

"Is it Thursday already?" I said.

"Are you daft?" said Nut.

"She *is* daft and that's only half of it," said Eliza.

"I'm teasing, Nut," I said. "And yes, Mrs. Wiggins, I'll get your tea."

I were not uplifted in spirit. With good reason, as it turned out. Simply said, he did not come to meet me. I waited. I fretted. I walked a bit around the square, but I knew already it were no use. I saw the pin girl and smiled, though I were sick with dismay. I made up all the reasons, as the hour ended and I headed back: Unexpected, he were kept in the stable. He were ill in some manner. Jacob Vickers had snitched and Caden had been punished on my behalf.

I would not yet permit myself to consider other possibilities.

"I'm back early because I've got a bit of a sore throat," I explained to Mrs. Wiggins. "But here's your tea."

Eliza raised an eyebrow in my direction, first time she'd looked my way all week. But that were all. An eyebrow.

Friday. Saturday. I scrubbed, peeled, hauled, and

sliced. Saturday night, Bates sent Nut to fetch a leather hide from the tanner, wanting to mend bucket handles and patch the driver's seat on the carriage.

"Ssst, Nut," I said as he were getting his jacket on. "I've an errand for you too."

He cocked his flappy ear and listened while I told him the least I could but enough; there were a young man hadn't kept a promise and I'd be most obliged if he'd stop by the stable to inquire over his state of health. It were close enough to the tannery that he could do it quick-like.

"Sure enough," said Nut. "And if I find him, I won't half tell him what I think of anyone letting down our Mary."

"Shhh, Nut. Keep it under, will you?" I lifted his cap and swiped his head. He winked at me, conspiring.

An hour passed, and eventually back he come, his cap pulled low. No one else bothered to look at him but I saw right off he had a shiner. Lordy, he'd been walloped! He dropped the leather in Bates's lap, grimaced at me, and pointed to the cellar, where he disappeared at once.

"Oh, didn't I forget to bring up the . . ." I stopped. What single item could possibly be needed from below? No one were really listening. I started down, but Bates called me back.

"Mary," he said. "Come here."

I stood by, feet jiggling.

Bates crooked his finger at me, made me bend over to hear his whisper. "Is there a boy needs whipping, Mary?"

That startled me upright. "What, Nut? No, Mr. Bates,

he's a good—" I were confused, knowing the poor boy had already had his eye blacked.

Bates yanked me back so I could feel his breath too close on my ear. "I don't mean the brat." That set a flush prickling up my neck like a wool scarf.

Worse, Eliza were on us. "Save it for elsewhere," she said. There were trouble brimming in her eyes. She were laying the tea trays, Cook were rolling pastry, I were meant to be spooning Master Sebastian's rice pudding into a dainty little bowl called a ramekin.

"Have you had any more news from home, Mary?" asked Eliza.

"You know I haven't."

"I suppose that stepmother would greet any good news of yours with surprise and great delight? Last Lane Cottage, was it? Pinchbeck?"

This is the minute she chooses?

"Currants," I said, pulling away from Bates. "Master Sebastian does like currants in his pudding."

I near flew to the cellar. Nut were at the bottom of the steps, his bashed-up face peering out of the dark.

"Oh, Nut, what's happened to you?"

"Come 'ere," he said. "I've got to tell you."

Did I want to know? "Did you see him?"

"I saw him, and I hate to say what I saw, miss, I'm that sorry for you."

I sank to sit on the bottom step. "Just tell me, Nut. We've only a minute."

"He was . . ."

Not kissing someone else, please, not that!

"He was *drunk,* miss, terrible drunk."

Much better! "How . . . ? Where did you . . . ?"

"I asked at the barracks, in the stable there's a man named Cleves, and he told me, 'Tucker's not here, try the Rose and Crown,' but at the Rose they told me they sent away the soldiers for being rowdy, miss."

"Rowdy? So where did you find him?"

"He was being carried by his mates, out of the Sailor's Delight. They were yelling at him, 'Tucker! Shut it!' But he was yelling back something awful."

"Yelling what?"

"Didn't catch all of it, not being close enough. His sisters, he said, they'd be wishing him dead."

"His *sisters?*"

"Then I went over, and I said, 'Mr. Tucker?' and he said, 'Who's asking?' 'I've got a message from Miss Finn, sir,' only then his mates beat me around the head, saying I was the cause of all his troubles. I told them no I wasn't. Mr. Tucker fell over and said he was cursed and who would tell his mother? His mates told him that's the way it is with women, they love you till you feel cursed. Then I skedaddled and come home."

My blood took to pounding in my earholes. I could only pat Nut and murmur, "Thank you, go off now," before I put my forehead against the stone cellar wall to cool my brain. Caden Tucker were full of shame, that much

were clear. Scared as a bunny . . . Facing those sisters of
his with his head up straight, telling them about me . . .
Were he willing to cast me off so easy? Were it all a trick,
us being sweethearts? It seemed real to me, but . . . what
did I know? Nothing I learned in Pinchbeck made sense
here. But for him to pretend I weren't even . . . just so's he
could look his family in the eye . . .

If I could have sunk lower than the bottom step, I'd
have done it.

JAMES 1888

Using the Tree

That new nurse had told him, "Go straight to the ward and stay there." If James missed supper, he'd be almost obeying. It was Sunday, so Mr. Byrd would be occupied with the evening service. James could be occupied with finding his mother at Mr. Byrd's home.

Every boy at the Foundling Hospital knew where the chaplain lived, even if they'd never seen it. Thanks to the chaplain's partially lame and entirely whimsical sister, the Byrd house was famous for flocks of her carved birds adorning the windowsills and perched along the edge of the roof. Rumor said that each time the chimney sweep came for his monthly visit, she paid him pennies extra to install her new creations.

James was certain that he could find such a house

without any trouble, knowing it was close enough that Miss Ada Byrd walked—limped—to the Foundling chapel on Sunday mornings. He'd seen her there, with a hickory cane and wind-mottled cheeks, though he had never been close enough to discover whether the boys' imitations were accurate. They claimed she warbled such comments as "My dear brother has his congregation, and I have mine . . . ," talking about the wooden birds.

He would find out tonight. He would see his mother and see the birds.

He climbed the tree. He inched his way along the branch, further than he'd gone before, not liking how it wobbled under him. The height from the top of the wall was greater than it had seemed before, now that he prepared to drop. Up there, he was still shielded by leaves, but as soon as he let go there would be no more hiding. Maybe he should wait until dark? No, finding the Byrd home meant seeing the birds, and that meant *before* dark. But still he hesitated. He hadn't been outside the gates in nearly five years. Things were different out there. Even the way they talked was different.

"Fresh and tasty, buy them hasty! Pies!"

Pie Peter! Someone he knew. Almost a friend. James held his breath and jumped, *whooft,* landing hard on his bum and an elbow. *Ouch!* But *no* crying! He scrambled up and dusted off. He shouldn't look as though he'd just escaped over a wall, should he? That made him smile, despite the scrapes. He was out!

Out, and in the middle of it! It was . . . like nothing he'd ever seen, except in glimpses from his branch. James imagined that the inside of the monkey man's music box might sound this way, with songs and clatter and cries chittering from every side. And *motion* wherever he looked: wheels hammering, horses clopping, bodies bumping, mouths hollering, chewing, laughing, kissing, spitting . . .

"Savory pies! Fresh and tasty!"

James had missed supper. The smell of the meat pies was enough to make a hungry boy dizzy. No wonder those urchins had staged a raid. But that kind of stealing was beyond him. He gazed at the basket, seeing glints of golden crust between folds of grease-spotted paper. He had not seen or sniffed any sort of food he'd actually *wanted* to eat since he was six years old.

"Hey! What are you gawpin' at?" Pie Peter was shaking his cap at James. "Get off with you, I've had enough of thieving boys!"

"I'm not a thief!" said James. "I want . . . I want a pie."

"Have you got a penny?" asked the old man. "Aha, I thought not! No penny, no pie. Get off with you!"

James slunk away, stomach churning.

There was a girl about his size against the wall. At least, James thought she was a girl. She wore a skirt, of sorts, though it seemed mended badly and was creased with grime. Her face was so filthy that Matron would have taken one look and fainted dead away. James hadn't spoken to a girl since his little sisters. She was staring at him, though, with dark, needing eyes.

"What?" said James.

"What yerself," she said, and sniffed. Her stare slid over James's jacket and down to his shoes.

Coram's bones! thought James. He didn't look right for being out there. It was the stupid uniform. He looked like . . . a foundling. He tore off the jacket and rolled it into a bundle that he clenched between his knees. His shirt was so clean it just about shone. With a shudder, he scooped a fistful of muck from the gutter and smeared it over his sleeves. He undid the tie and crumpled it up.

The dirty girl studied every move.

"What?" said James.

"What yerself."

"Go away," said James.

"Go away yerself."

James turned his back, tucked the jacket under his arm, and moved along the wall away from the Hospital's front gates. It began to drizzle, melting the mud splotches on his sleeves to a more even brown. The girl stayed right behind him. James stopped. He threw down his red tie and watched her pounce.

"You can have it," he said. She kept watching him while she knotted it around her own neck. Then she lunged, surprising him, snatching at the jacket. James held on but she had a good grip and kept yanking in sharp tugs.

"Hey! Stop it!" James hoped one of those hurrying

gentlemen would come to his aid, but no. The girl had one of the brass buttons now, twisting it hard until suddenly she tumbled backward, button in hand. James laughed, she looked so astonished, sitting there with her legs sticking out. There were no soles on her boots! She scowled and hauled herself up, waving the button at him before racing away.

Was that what she'd wanted all along? The buttons? They were shiny and gold-colored, each imprinted with a little lamb, the symbol of the Hospital. Maybe out here, buttons could work the way sweets did on the other side of the wall? Thinking of sweets, James felt the jacket cuffs and found two. One for now and one for later. He turned the jacket wrong way out and put it on again, with the buttons pressing against his chest.

ELIZA 1878

Seeks Out Mr. Tucker

Eliza could see that Mary was shaken up terrible. She was sneaking around, having secret outings, whispering with Bates in full view of everyone, never smiling—not even at Nut, though he seemed to be part of the mystery. She certainly wasn't her cheery self—well, who would be?

All the times it might have been Eliza! She'd been grateful before, but now . . . What wouldn't she give to be in Mary's place? That was worth considering, wasn't it? If Eliza could get Mary safely elsewhere, she just might play the very same game in pursuit of Harry Bates.

So, what or who might be prevailed upon to take on Mary Finn? Hope and intrigue and wiliness popped up like blisters after a spilt kettle. Eliza would not sit about

waiting for an act of thievery where her man was concerned. She'd got fresh vigor in her mission, and Mr.
Tucker would soon be feeling it!

It was most gratifying to see the soldiers' eyes brighten
at the sight of her. This was like a good deed, a *duty*,
even, for a girl to spread a bit of charm about for these
poor young men. *Starved*, they likely were, for a glimpse
of a girl's curvy bits not to mention a kiss and a cuddle. Not
that she was here to do any kissing, but Eliza was certain
that even just *looking* at a healthy lass would give these
boys a reason to fight a little fiercer for England.

"Now, there's a peach I'd like to take a bite of!" one fellow called out.

"A pair of peaches!" shouted another. This caused
quite a chorus of remarks, going decidedly off-color. Possibly not the most *refined* regiment, thought Eliza. She'd
best snag her quarry and depart quickly.

"Can I help you, miss?" It was an older, grizzly chap, a
servant.

"I'm looking for Mr. Tucker, if you please. Just for a
minute."

"In there." The man pointed to the stable. "But!" He
held up a hand to stop her. "The men aren't permitted lady
visitors dropping by willy-nilly."

"Oh. Well," said Eliza, "I'm not a lady. I mean, I am a
lady, of course, but I'm his cousin, too. Eliza Pigeon."

"His cousin, is it?" The man scratched his chin so hard

his tongue slid out over his lower lip. "Funny as how they've got so many sisters and cousins."

So she wasn't the first to use that ploy. What a disgusting man! Eliza wished she had a coin to sweeten him with. She adjusted her bodice instead.

"I'll let you have your minute, miss. But I'll need to be keeping an eye out for nonsense." He tipped his head for her to follow him into the stable, setting off a new round of hooting from the lingering soldiers.

Mr. Tucker was down a few stalls, brushing a horse. How did anyone work in a place that reeked so?

"I've brought your *cousin,* Mr. Tucker." The man leaned against an open bin full of straw. "You do recall your cousin? Miss, uh, Miss Pigeon?"

The young man certainly remembered her. His cheeks went all pink and his eyes skipped about like he'd been caught looking. "Of course," he said. "Thank you, Mr. Cleves. Cousin, dear. How is your injured ankle?"

"Quite healed, thank you." Would the nasty man just stand there?

"And your purse? In good health as well?"

Eliza couldn't help but laugh. He was a pretty one, that was a fact, but nervous as a chased bird. No wonder Mary was still only on nodding terms with him—he was afraid of women!

"Is . . . has something happened?" His voice dropped low. "Miss Finn . . . is . . . also in good health?"

"The thing is, Mr.—Cousin—that Miss Finn's got herself into some trouble."

He looked quite ill, now that she leaned closer in the gloom of the stable.

His eyes darted over to where the Cleves chap was now chewing on straw. "I wouldn't know," Mr. Tucker said, hasty-like. "I hardly know her." He shrugged, offering half a smile.

"I just wondered if she'd be a girl you might fancy?" Eliza waited for a nod or a blush, praying that he'd consider himself a suitor and entice Mary away from Bates. But no, he stared off at one of the horses, his face plain and mouth slack. She had an idea, though.

"I was wondering," said Eliza, quiet as she could, "if perhaps you'd like to know her better?"

He blinked. How could it hurt if she tried out a version of the truth?

"I'll be honest with you. She's got herself mixed up with a fellow in the house, you see. Someone who was promised to me. And so I thought, well, if you—"

"Hey," said Cleves. "What's all the whispering?"

Mr. Tucker was staring at her, blank-eyed, as if she were speaking like a Chinaman.

"I can see I was mistaken. A flirty one like Mary doesn't appeal to all kinds."

Now he reddened up. "A fellow in the *house*? On Neville Street?" His head was wagging, surprised-like.

She should stop now. But "Yes, and he's *my* fellow. I don't foretell a happy ending."

"She's . . . in *trouble*?" he said. "She . . . she doesn't look it, but maybe she *is* trouble." His face twitched a little, like he was holding a sneeze. "I . . . no . . . I wouldn't want, well, some fellow's leftovers."

"No, I can see that." Disappointment ached in Eliza's throat. "It's no concern of yours."

"No concern of mine."

He walked her to the stable door, with as dull a face as ever she'd seen. Perhaps he was stupid after all.

MARY 1878

Seeks Out Mr. Tucker

We servants went to the Sunday service, same as the family did, always scurrying home to put the luncheon on the table. Lady A. were ever so urgent about having an elegant Sunday luncheon, though the embarrassment of Miss Lucilla living here with her husband elsewhere meant no one were invited except theirselves and Miss Hollow.

Sundays, apart from those minutes in church, were as busy as any other day, but the supper was a light one. I were watching out for a minute to call my own, but it were Eliza who disappeared while Nut and I did the washing up and scoured the pots. I must have spoken to Caden ten times an hour inside my head, from haughty to pleading and back again. I only wanted a chance to say a few words to his face. But all of Monday went grinding by and most of Tuesday with me spitting prayers at Heaven there'd be a reason I'd be sent out.

Finally, an hour before supper, Cook sighed. "Find us some fresh cress, will you, Mary? The girl who comes round this way must grow hers on a dung heap." I were out the door before I'd blinked.

The barracks and the street were near empty, where usually they were crowded with soldiers. I made myself go into the stable and found the man Cleves. I inquired could I see Mr. Tucker and he were smirking and uppity, said I should speak to an officer.

"An officer?" I said. "I only want to see Mr. Tucker for a minute."

"Third door from the end," said Cleves.

The interview behind third-door-from-the-end were a short one. It does not take long, after all, for a man to crush a girl's heart to sawdust.

I couldn't remember, after, how I'd explained my quest. His words, though, are chiseled deep in me, said patient-like and slow like I were slow myself.

"I'm sorry, miss. He requested that he be shipped out with the battalion. They departed yesterday for Afghanistan. We've got a column going through the Khyber Pass to Jellalabad."

He were using foreign words but the intent were clear.

"I believe you've been disappointed by your young man . . ." Him sniggering, no doubt, behind his mustache, while my hopes tumbled straight through to my boot soles, not pausing in the middle where the cause of it all were churning me up.

JAMES 1888

Finds Shelter

The sharp, sweet lemon drop cheered James up. He'd better move more quickly; the rain had hurried dusk. The night and the fog were dancing, each trying to put a foot down first. He'd walk the whole way around the Hospital grounds, keeping a sharp lookout for anyone familiar. If he still hadn't found the chaplain's house, he'd widen the circle, street by street. It couldn't be too far. Miss Byrd managed to walk the distance with a cane!

James ducked from doorway to doorway until he was too wet to care. There were so many streets! And so many people! He arrived back at the Hospital's main gates, gloomy and sodden. But, *Coram's knuckles,* he saw policemen! Two bobbies were marching up the drive and two more were speaking with the porter, Mr. Travers. Was this because of James? They'd called in the police force?

He slipped behind a stall with a painted sign, DUBIE'S WELL-MADE BROOMS. The man shooed him off with one of his meager brushes.

"Hah!" shouted James. "You call these brooms?" As a second-former, he was a broom expert. He'd made much finer! He ducked and tore away as Dubie came thwacking after him.

He watched from a doorway, only steps further along. A small crowd of dark figures clustered at the porter's booth, but it was too dim to see who they were. Behind the gates, the castle of the Hospital loomed, lights twinkling in some windows, but mostly dark. The children were in their beds by seven o'clock and it must be far past that now. When had they missed James? They'd had their supper, they'd washed, been tormented, said their prayers, and climbed into their cots. Walter would be fretting next to the empty bed. Frederick would pretend not to care. He'd likely pretend he'd helped with the escape.

There were men with lanterns assembled at the gate. They were coming to look for him, he knew it. But he hadn't found Mama Peevey yet, so he could not be found himself.

James blinked away his tears. His head was heavier than his neck could bear. He crept into a narrow lane between two houses, all the way to the end. He stamped his feet at the scooting shadows and found the entrance to a cellar, half covered by a brick archway. On his knees, he groped about in the blackness, collecting rags and newspapers that littered the alley. He laid them down across a step and made himself a nest.

ELIZA 1878

Mary Cracks

It gave Eliza a nip of pleasure to see Mary blubbering when she come back that day. Had she been to visit one of those women who could flush a baby? And been told a price too high? Or had her new friend Mr. Tucker hurled a few stinging words in her direction, finally armed with the truth?

Nut, the baffled little squirt, kept tugging on Mary's arm, saying, "Miss, why're you crying, miss? Miss!" until Eliza stepped in and gave him a swat. That swat got Mary's notice.

"Do not *ever* touch him again!" Her finger stabbed at Eliza. She looked half barmy.

"Mary!" Mrs. Wiggins did not tolerate the use of emotions in her kitchen. "Whatever's troubling you, it needs to get packed away. Have you got my cress?"

"No, Mrs. Wiggins," said Mary, calm-like for a moment.

"I did not stop for the cress, as my life were ending." With that, she started up the stairs. With a blotched face and hair all thataway!

"Miss!" called Nut. "Where are you going?"

"Hell," she called back. "Straight to hell."

"Whatever has got into her?" Cook was right bewildered.

"I'll tell you," said Eliza, finally bursting out with it. "*Bates* has got into her. And left something behind, if you take my meaning."

Oh, what a pleasure to say it aloud!

Only not realizing the effect.

"Here!" cried Nut. "Help me!" He had both hands on Mrs. Wiggins, steering her swooning body into a chair.

"That was quick, Nut. Good work." Eliza flapped a tea towel in front of the cook's face.

Mrs. Wiggins blinked and pressed a hand over her heart.

"I'm off," Eliza whispered to Nut. "You stay with her and I'll find Mary."

"Don't you tell any more lies," said Nut. But Eliza was clattering up the stairs and didn't bother to answer. Where did the hussy think she was going, looking half-crazy? Not to their attic room by way of the front stairs, so what was she after? This was utterly . . . *gripping*. The heat of it, the *fun*, was like a rash on Eliza, racing along her arms and up her neck.

Then, whoa! She skidded to a stop on the second

landing. Mary was there, as distraught as she'd been below. But Miss Lucilla was there too, with Bates carrying in her purchases. They all three looked at Eliza, arriving as she did with a bit of a bump.

"Has this household gone mad?" said Miss Lucilla. "Why are you standing about, Mary? And so . . . *disarranged?*"

"I've been looking for you, Mrs. Overly. I need to speak to you, private-like."

"Mary," said Bates, gentle and worried.

"For Sebastian's sake," Mary added, ignoring him.

Eliza gaped at Mary's gall. The words of the handbook flew into her mind: *Never begin to talk to the mistress unless it is to deliver a message or to ask a necessary question.*

Miss Lucilla glance around, blank as usual, seeming disconcerted to have three servants looming, expecting something from her.

But, tugging at her gloves, she rose to the moment. "Mary, take my parcels from Mr. Bates and bring them into my room." She led the way.

Bates placed the packages in Mary's arms as though he were handing over an infant. Eliza let out an exasperated gust of breath.

"Mary." Bates was urgent. "You shouldn't be here."

She grasped the parcels and turned tail, flouncing almost. Eliza reached out to touch Bates's sleeve but he shook her off as if she were Nut.

OLIVER 1888

James Is Missing

From the window of his classroom, Oliver could see straight down the drive, over the gates and beyond to the London night. Torches burned, gaslights flickered, occasional braziers glowed, roasting chestnuts or birds on spits. The constellations winking from Heaven were mirrored on the city streets.

Nothing duller than an amateur poet, thought Oliver, turning away from the window, reaching for his hat.

Right away he looked out again, in case that was the instant there might appear a small boy, a smudge slightly darker than the surrounding city. But no. The cluster of men at the gate was still assembling, no sign of a discovery or celebration. He'd better hurry to join them.

He pressed his forehead and fingertips against the

window, spectacles clinking as glass met glass. *I'm a coward.* There came a flare of light below as another torch was lit. *A ten-year-old boy is braver than I am, plunging into that hive.*

There were many allusions to insects, living in the midst of a city: swarms, hordes, drones, buzzing . . . but that wasn't what unnerved Oliver. Every one of the lights out there had been lit by a person, a person from a family, a person with a story, with connections and memories.

Oliver shook himself.

How had James got out, anyway? The *why* was clear. He'd gone to find his mother. But Mrs. Peevey rested only a few streets away, and James had never arrived.

Where are you, boy?

Which was worse: that James should be missing or that Oliver must step out into the dark street? Oliver hustled to the door. Losing James, of course.

MARY 1878

Tells About a Proposal

Wouldn't you know it, Eliza were there to witness my downfall. Bates scowled at me too. *So he knows,* I thought. *Eliza has ruined me.*

No, I have ruined myself.

Miss Lucilla directed me to put her packages on the bureau. I returned to pull the door firmly shut. She removed her hat and dropped the pins into the porcelain tray on the vanity. I were shivering in my dismay. She took off her jacket and shook it gently before laying it over the back of a chair.

"Well?" she said.

"Miss."

"You have something to say that concerns my son?"

Oh, I'd mentioned that, hadn't I? *Go on!*

"He's a fine boy," I said. "He's growing up very bonny."

"What is it, then, Mary? I've been shopping on Regent Street for hours. I'm quite worn out."

It were wrong to push. She were never too bright, which had slipped my distressed mind.

"Oh, miss!" Tears at once prickled my eyes.

"For Heaven's sake! What's this? Hardy little Mary?"

I had perhaps a minute before her patience would expire. I gulped for air and confidence.

"I'm in trouble, Miss Lucilla. Terrible trouble, the way you were when we first met, but worse, of course, because I have no home to go to, no waiting mam to rescue me. And I weren't wed, though we planned to, I swear it, and now at any minute I'll be sent away—"

"*What* are you saying?"

"I'm asking for help, miss. I know I don't deserve it except that I helped you, did I not? I came to Neville Street at your particular request, for Master Sebastian."

She stared at me with eyebrows pinched, still vague on my predicament. Her mind had not fastened to the story as quickly as I would wish.

"Are you saying that you wish to marry your young man?"

"I wish it with all my heart!" Once again I began to cry, to the point my lips were salty. "But he has gone away! And I am left . . . I am left"—I could barely whisper—"with child."

She jumped away as if I'd poked her with a needle. "Mary, no!"

I tried to muffle foolish sobs with hands against my face, scraping for breath. Finally, "I am applying to you, Miss Lucilla, as a woman who knows how it feels to be . . . lost—"

She cut me off. "There is nothing I can do for you." Her reedy voice were as calm as a curtain over a closed window. "You have made the gravest of mistakes. I would not have you under the same roof as my son. Mrs. Wiggins cannot act quickly enough to put you out. To protect us all. Good day."

She couldn't have hurt me worse if she'd struck me. I were lower than a worm's belly, as you can imagine. I got myself out of her room, through an oddly empty kitchen, and down as far as the cellar steps. And there I sat shivering, quite dazed.

The railing were cold, my bum were cold, my feet were cold. Too cold to hold me up. If I tried to stand, I'd tumble down these stairs and break my neck. It'd all be over in one snap. Now, wouldn't that be a perfect solution? But falling down the steps might not be certain enough. With my luck, it'd be a leg or a wrist instead of my neck, and then what? If I were going to toss myself somewhere, the River Thames would be the place. I shivered. It'd be cold. It were full of floating muck that I'd have to swallow first.

Now, if I were considering swallowing something? Poison were easier than drowning, no question. There must be all manner of poisons in the kitchen. I wouldn't want one that bloated me up or turned me blue, though. That were a stopping point, actually. The idea of Eliza— and it would most likely be Eliza . . . the idea of her being the one to peel off my dress and my underthings, to lay me out and to handle my body . . . and what if she needed help? Would she ask Nut? That would horrify the poor boy.

I had a wee cry thinking of Nut's bony shoulders hunched over my deadness and knew I couldn't do that. Worse would be Bates. Those big sassy hands on me would irk Eliza something awful.

The door above me opened just then, as my mind were blithering. Light spilled down, reminding me how wedged I were on the narrow steps.

"I'm all right, Nut," I said, feeling his shadow, not turning around. "You're not to worry. I'm only having a . . . quiet minute."

"We've been looking for you."

I jumped. It were Bates, not Nut, and his voice woke me up like dropping an ice chip down my bodice.

"Oh!" I hustled to my feet. "I were just . . ." What excuse could there be for me hiding on the cellar steps?

"Mary," he said. "You're to be out of this house within the hour." He weren't fierce or sarcastic, simply making certain I knew my lot.

I nodded.

"Unless . . . ," he said.

I were facing him now, two or three steps below him.

He were a dark figure looming over me, with the lit kitchen behind.

"Don't you dare, Mr. Bates," I said, grabbing at the railing, suddenly sure he were intent on pushing me down to the very fate I'd just been fancying for myself.

"What?" He reached toward me and I bit his hand as hard as if it were a nutshell.

"Ow! What are you doing, woman?" He jerked his hand out of my mouth, making my teeth clack as I tasted, what was it? Linseed?

"Let me past," I hissed at him, pushing against his belt. I blushed, it being a mortification where my nose would meet his trousers, placed as I were on the stair. He caught my angry fists in his hands, laughing. Laughing! "Clear off, Bates!" I struggled. "Don't you lay a finger on me! No one's got a right—"

"Dammit, Mary, I've been hunting you all over this house. I want to say something before you leave, before you go running away like a—"

There were a note in his voice that I'd not heard before. It were most unexpected, because it sounded like kindness.

"Mary, you're in terrible trouble."

"Ha," I said. "That's not news to me!"

"I can help, you daft girl! Would you just listen?"

"Help? By offing me down the kitchen stairs?"

"By marrying you," he said.

I'd have been less surprised if he'd struck my face. I

lost my footing and teetered to one side, heaving against
the railing and grateful for his quick arms that caught me
up and near carried me into the kitchen and put me in a
chair.

He ran a finger along the plate rail by the cellar door
and knocked a key to the ground. He winked, and had
Mrs. Wiggins's brandy cupboard opened and closed before you could say *Mary Finn has lost her sense,* holding a
bottle and soon tipping it to half-fill a teacup.

"Drink," he said, and I obeyed. He took a quick glug
from the bottle itself and put it back where it lived. He
pulled up the fire stool and stared into my face, taking a
breath and then talking urgent, like there were not a
heartbeat to waste.

"You don't like me, Mary Finn, I know that, but I am
offering to save your life. I will marry you and make things
right. We could keep working here, or go away, if you
wanted, find a situation in the country . . ."

He were the very last person I expected to speak in a
soft voice, the very last I ever thought would have a com-
passionate thought or who could conceive an action of
such tenderness.

I burst into tears and let him hold me up with those
arms that Eliza did go on about.

JAMES 1888

What James Could See

James was curled up so tight in the morning he thought he mightn't *uncurl*, arms locked around his knees, neck and back all cricked and achy . . . he'd slept a bit but his body stayed scared just in case. Light trembled at the end of the alley: a bright morning, not foggy and dismal.

He blinked and stayed still.

WHAT HE COULD SEE WITHOUT MOVING:
- *Quite a pile of rags, stiff and crusted with mud*
- *Heaps of old newspapers, sodden and melted together*
- *A bucket without its bottom*
- *Broken milk bottles*
- *Ever so many pamphlets, splattered and torn, blown every which way, and all announcing:*

Dramatic Entertainment
Theatre Royal
The
Vampire
or
Bride of the Isles
6 nights with
Miss Ellen Devere
as the Maiden

- *A dead bird, no, two dead birds, necks . . . snapped? With wings flung wide as if still gliding.*

James leaned over, poking gently at the feathers with a rag.

- *A few rotted potatoes and rusted lettuces*

Hungry as he was, these were not close to edible. Even the morning gruel at the Foundling, or, better yet, the thick-cut bread with a smear of butter . . . James hiccupped a small laugh, thinking of Mr. Byrd and his telling them always to be grateful. Bread and butter were something to be grateful for, after all. He sat up, wiggling his toes and flapping his fingers.

WHAT HE COULD SEE WITH HIS EYES CLOSED:

- *Rosie, bigger than he'd thought about her being, hair still so straggly that her pigtails were only as thick as pencils. But that look on her face when she'd cried out, "James!"*
- *Could he remember Lizzy if he squeezed tight his eyes to find a picture? There she was, sticking out her tongue in triumph, swiping the last biscuit. . . .*
- *Mr. Chester silhouetted at the window of the history classroom, spectacles glinting, voice low and full of . . . of daring, while he told the tale of a king's execution or a captain's sighting America.*
- *Mama Peevey's bright eyes and arms held wide . . .*

Only what was the matter with her now?

ELIZA 1878

Hears a Proposal

Naturally, Eliza had scooted up the stairs after Mary, ever keen to discover, *What now?* She wasn't surprised to find Bates lurking—when wasn't he, these days? But fancy Mary swanning into Miss Lucilla's bedchamber, as if she'd every right! And no chance for Eliza to hear a single word because along came Miss Hollow, wondering where was Master Sebastian's supper tray? So Eliza had to quick make and bring up his boiled egg and rice pudding, all on her own as the kitchen was empty. But she paid no mind as she was eager to get back to lingering outside Miss Lucilla's door. Only, Miss Hollow said, "Now that you're here, you may wipe down the blinds as I've been asking for a fortnight."

Eliza didn't think fast enough to put off that dreary

task, so wasted half an hour in the nursery. She hustled down after, fearing that Mary would be packed and gone before she could get a last word in. Still no sign of Mrs. Wiggins, nor Bates, nor even that creeping little monster Nut. So what had happened to Mary? Eliza would have gone looking but for a noise from the cellar stairwell. Whoever . . . ? Ah, it was *them*. Eliza hovered next to the crack in the door.

"Mary," Bates was saying. "You're in terrible trouble."

"Ha," said the trollop. "That's not news to me!"

Eliza hovered next to the crack in the door, pressing a palm over her heart so's its thumping couldn't be heard.

"I can help, you daft girl! Would you just listen?"

She *was* daft! About time he noticed!

"Help? By offing me down the kitchen stairs?"

"By marrying you," he said.

Eliza would have fallen right over, but her feet were canny enough to get her across the floor and out to the street.

MARY 1878

Telling About Disaster

Now it seemed that the hands on the clock were somehow spinning faster and noisier than usual. Nut shot through the door with Cook on his tail, stopping short when they spied me and Bates, though thankfully we had finished our embrace, as my husband-to-be had quite a scent up close. Mrs. Wiggins wore such a scowl you'd think I'd killed the best rooster.

"Here you are," she said. "We've been looking."

"Here I am," I said, eyes down, trying for respectful.

"I didn't think you'd last a week when you came here, Mary. You won me over with hard work and that smile of yours. And now you've let me down, getting yourself in trouble like this. I'm downright disappointed, but you're to gather up your belongings and be off."

"You needn't go rushing down that road after all, Mrs. Wiggins," said Bates. "We're getting married, me and Mary, so there'll be no call to send her away."

I were relieved that Eliza were not there to hear him declare our intentions. Still, what happened instead mayhap were worse. Mrs. Wiggins clutched at her bosom as if struck by a bullet. She wheezed into a chair and went trembly. But it were Nut, gasping and throwing hisself at me, that shook me awake.

"No! Miss!" His face puckered up like a colicky baby. "You can't do that! Not Bates!" Those little arms enwrapped my waist with the fiercest grip.

"Hey!" Bates jumped on the boy, wrenching him off me by the scruff of the neck and throwing him onto the floor. Cook were huffing, I were shrieking, and Nut were crying most pitiful. Bates gave Nut a kick, and that were it. I hauled back my foot and kicked Bates as hard as I could.

"What the *hell* are you doing, girl?"

"I wouldn't marry you now if you paid me in gold," I said.

"Enough!" shouted Mrs. Wiggins. "We do not live in Bedlam! Mr. Bates, kindly remove yourself to the yard. Mary Finn, pack your bag. And, Nut . . . Lord love me, Nut?"

Bates stamped out while I knelt down next to Nut, him lying in a bundle by the stove. "You hurt anywhere, Nut?"

He looked up with bruised eyes and his nose a-dribbling. "No, miss." He pulled me low so's he could whisper. "Don't you worry about me, miss. I'm a tough one, right?"

"Yes, Nut, that's certain."

"But you can't marry Bates, miss. He's not good. Go, miss. Please, just go!"

I turned on my toes and went upstairs, skin prickling, heart racing, baby jumping. It were only two minutes later that Eliza flung herself in, glowering something awful.

I'd have liked to tell Eliza that I were not going to marry her beau after all, but that would have meant telling her I'd been close to doing it. The satisfaction didn't seem worth the trouble. She were looking everywhere but in my face, her eyes most curious about my belly. She stood in the doorway with her arms strapped across her chest like guns.

I gathered my belongings into my shawl, meager pile that it were. Thinking that word, *belongings,* made my throat ache. "Belonging" were far from suitable.

"Mrs. Wiggins said to watch you don't steal anything."

"You know I won't."

"I don't know."

"We've been sleeping bum to bum for how many months?" I said. "Do you really think I'd take the soap? Or the blanket? I've *been* your blanket some nights, Eliza."

"You're a liar and a slut so why not a thief too?"

"You know I'm not."

"I don't know."

"If . . . if it were you . . . in trouble," I started.

"It's not," she said, but only, we both knew, by the merest chance.

"It weren't Bates," I said. I tied a knot with the corners

of the shawl. She were staring at me peculiar, like she expected more.

"May I pass, please?"

She looked down at her chapped hands.

"Eliza?"

Her mind were rumbling to find a clever retort, to scratch me with words so's I'd leave bleeding.

"If you want to see the last of me," I said, "you will have to let me go through the door."

She stepped aside.

Mrs. Wiggins waited in the kitchen, no Bates to be seen. Her mouth were a ribbon of disappointment.

"You're off?"

"Yes, Mrs. Wiggins."

"Show me."

I unknotted the corners of my shawl and let her look. No soap. No currants. No ink. No nothing.

"Mrs. Wiggins? I . . . I . . . have nowhere to go. I don't know what . . . I . . ."

"You have called down these troubles upon your own head, Mary. The rules were simple. I . . . I'm sorry . . . I did think you were a good girl."

"But, Mrs. Wiggins, I am! It were . . . I loved him! And he loved me."

She shook her head, sad as can be. "Do you think that matters to anyone, Mary? Love is not for the likes of us, belowstairs."

Nut were waiting on the step, in particular to be the

last face I saw at Neville Street. He were pale and tearful, cheeks streaked and shoulders shuddering. He clasped me about the middle and would have stayed there a week except that Mrs. Wiggins came out on the step and dragged him inside. So that were that. I were crumbly all through, and couldn't think later how I'd done it, but I walked away down Neville Street with as straight a back as I could manage. At the corner I turned, and saw Eliza at the attic window. I raised my hand, one last wave, but she ducked her head and pulled the shutter to.

Truth or Lie?

There were too many pieces for Eliza to have a hold on all of them.

Was Bates the *father* of this calamity? Or not? And if not, then why the *devil* was he making an offer of marriage to someone he'd called a *mere child*? Hadn't Eliza written out the words *Mrs. Harry Bates* at least one hundred times? Shouldn't all that frolicking lead somewhere substantial? Didn't she deserve to feel a little pique under the circumstances?

And if—by some chance—she'd got things wrong, how could Eliza ever confess that she had gone to see Mr. Tucker? That she'd told him . . . That if it weren't for her . . . That Mary's plight was all on account of a terrible mistake?

Not that Mary could be trusted, with those cunning

green eyes and rosy lips. She was likely still fibbing every time she breathed. Better to remember that. Why worry where a liar might go from here? Better to chew over how to rekindle vigor in Bates. If he were willing to be married, he only needed guidance as to the choice of wife. If being a hero was so almighty important, Eliza could—she counted back the weeks on her fingers—Eliza could easily develop a few of the same symptoms. All it took was a bit of puking . . .

MARY 1878

What Happened Next

May you never know the despair that colored those first hours after I took my leave from the Allyn house.

Like a thread in a laundry tub, I were adrift and tumbled amongst the blurring crowd. Not having a place to walk toward, I walked all anyhow, and meanwhile commenced my pleading straight to God. *Show me,* I begged. *I've not been demanding of your favor. You've got my mam, after all! Should you not be of some use in her place?* And what answer did I get? The closing in of fog all around, as if to recall the night of my first embrace with Caden, to point the finger back at me. *Thou hast misstepped!* God's voice in my head were a little too close to that Margaret Huckle's. Were it meant to invite me home?

Thomas and Davy would be pleased as a birthday to

see me. Wouldn't they? Only what if their stepmother had slipped her poison into their cups? What if little Nan sniffed at me, suspicious? But they'd be won over soon enough, I trusted that. It were our dad who'd sit between his wife and me, his heart forever pulled two ways at once. It niggled in me that I might not be the one to win such a contest, what with my rounded body and the steady drizzle of her opinion on his head.

And however could I hold up my chin on the threshold of that cottage, knowing there were no Small John waiting inside?

In my belly came a nudge as if a wee chick were discovering its beak. I stepped into the lee of a stall, mopping the fog drips from my face. If only Caden would appear right then and put his hands on me and warm my hips and scorch my face with kissing. But what use was such a fancy? Only to loose the tears. Should I intend to appear forlorn and sorrowful, to flaunt my plight, in hope of a tossed penny or the crust of a pie? Were it my destiny to finish up in the workhouse?

The workhouse sent my thinking skipping back to Nut's wee face, both eyes purpled now, thanks to Bates being rough. And thanks to Bates being rough on Nut, I were here a-sopping instead of making ready to be his bride. There weren't an hour went by I didn't reconsider those few stormy moments that skittered me out here.

Wed to Bates, I'd have held my position on Neville Street; it'd soon be forgot that you weren't his . . . Bates could have writ my father, we'd have had news that mended all tears, we might have gone to visit someday . . . Had I gone quite mad to depart from such a possibility as that?

But one quick think on Nut and I were sure that madness never clouded my reasoning. If Bates could kick one motherless boy, what might he do in a fit of anger to my own fatherless child? And if I closed my eyes and thought about him . . . kissing me, about his hands untying my apron, slipping under my skirt . . . it near about made me queasy.

It were Nut who saved me. Us really, me *and* you. *"Go, miss, just go!"* he'd cried. He were the one with love so swelling up his heart that he could send me off, only knowing the outcome must be better than what I nearly settled for. Well, Lordy, didn't he teach me something that day?

And all this while, it were fogging and then dripping and finally raining mournful hard. *Damn you, Caden Tucker. Damn you to Hell till your blue eyes burn!*

It were feeling shame from the cursing that brought to mind St. Pancras Church, only a few streets away. It were too grand, of a regular day, for a mite like me to enter so bold. But there I went and there I huddled through that night and another, in the darkest pew, and there my dress and shawl did finally dry, as if by the quiet winking of candlelight.

What happened next were the part in the story where

the princess is tied up in the dungeon with bats swoop-
ing and the executioner's footstep on the stairs . . . and all
the listeners draw in their breaths together, knowing the
end is hovering. But stories have a way of tricking you.
Perhaps it's not the sinister stranger in a dark hood at
all. . . .

In my case, it weren't the dashing prince, either, but
more of a wrinkly old angel. A carriage pulled to a stop
with a sloppy spray of water sogging my skirt, two days'
drying for naught. The driver paid no mind to me but got
down to open the door. It were an aged lady inside and she
looked at the muck beneath the wheels and stretched a
hand out to touch the drizzle. The driver were not her own,
I could see that. He were hired, and bored, and not so at-
tentive as he should be to a passenger who looked like a
ghost already. Her hair gleamed like gaslight through
gauze and her glove on the door were the palest lilac.

"Mr. Richards?"

But Mr. Richards might have been brother to Harry
Bates. He were busy eyeing two young ladies struggling
with their umbrella in such a way that their bosoms
bounced. The old lady had one foot on the step, expecting
the driver to be there. I come forward, damp as I were,
with an arm out to assist her. There were a second when
she and I shared a smile, knowing it were not my place
but she being grateful that someone were watching. It
were only a second because Mr. Richards chose to do his
job just then and trod on my foot as he turned, sending

me flat to my bum in the road. It were so sudden that I toppled right over and knocked my head with a nasty thump. The lady made an odd sort of scream but I were that winded that I lay like a pudding. Next thing, Mr. Richards were dragging me up and the lady were ordering him severely to bring me inside her house.

So there I were, bruised and bedraggled, on a stool by the kitchen fire, listening to the old lady tell the tale to her companion.

"But, Aunt Kaye," said the younger woman, as though I were deaf. "You've invited a complete stranger into the house! How do you know she's not conspiring with the driver?"

"Conspiring? Dear girl, I've never heard such nonsense. Let's put the kettle on."

I believe the Misses Reed were what Eliza would call *refined,* meaning polite and posh. If their family had been rich long ago, now they were watching their pennies. They were Miss Kaye, the old lady, and her niece, Miss Angela. I arrived there scared as a rabbit with a snared foot. No hope, and yet still living.

The old lady were so kind that it near made me teary. I were sponged off and dried out, well fed with biscuits and tea, and my boots put near the grate to warm up. Miss Kaye Reed entertained us with an account of Mr. Richards's other missteps during the afternoon, ending with his treading on me. As the hour wore on, I carefully confessed that I were in need of a position.

"You wouldn't have to pay me wages," I said. "And I'm a good worker. I'd sleep in the kitchen and only need a little food."

Miss Angela Reed were thinking up plenty of objections, but Miss Kaye Reed said the kitchen were no place for an interview, and would I please come to the parlor.

She would write, she said, to Lord and Lady Allyn for my character, since it came out soon enough that I couldn't write for myself. She were sitting at her desk, which were a lovely dark wood, polished so it shone warm. It had a dozen little drawers with crystal knobs and a green blotter laid down. Miss Angela told me later it had belonged to her grandfather and it were their one "good piece." Miss Kaye stroked the edge with her thumb as if it were a cat.

"I shall hear back from the Allyns within a day or two and then we shall be all set, shan't we, Mary?" She "shalled" and "shan'ted" as if it were a special prayer. But she noticed that my reply weren't quick enough.

"Is there a reason you mightn't like me to write to the Allyns, Mary?"

My eyes were lowered, the way I'd learned from Eliza, not looking at her straight. Should I tell the truth or not? If I told a falsehood, would it tie me up further?

"Mary?"

I shrugged, which I knew at once to be the wrong thing.

"We don't like shrugging in this house, Mary. It signals laziness of mind. Look at me, my dear."

So I looked, and saw the watery eyes behind her spectacles and the soft creased skin of her face dotted with brown spots, like an apple in March at the bottom of the barrel. She seemed truly curious as to how I'd arrived upon the rose-splashed carpet beside her desk.

I would tell her.

"It won't help to write, Miss Reed."

Or some, anyway.

"And why is that, Mary?"

"They don't think much of my character at Allyn House," I said, very quiet. "Mrs. Wiggins, she's the cook you'd hear from, she turned me out, though I were the best worker she had; new, but I tried harder than Eliza any day of the week and especially on Mondays doing the washing."

"Was there trouble?"

My tongue were blubbery and dry at the same time. *Do I say? Do I lie? Do I save my own self?*

"I were . . . married . . . without asking, ma'am. I didn't know about permission. I didn't know it were wrong."

"Where is your husband now?"

Pretense over, I began to leak tears and showered the poor lady with my anguish.

"He's gone to Afghanistan! He's with the Ninth Battalion, gone to war!"

She held out a handkerchief and waited while I mopped my eyes and cleared the snot from my nose.

"My niece will not agree with me," she said, "but I am

old enough to trust my own judgment of the people I meet. We shall have a trial, you and I. You shall be put upon to prove that you are trustworthy, hardworking, and sober. I shall be put upon to prove that I am capable of assessing human nature. Does that suit you, Miss Mary Finn?"

I fell, yes, *fell* to my knees to thank her, queasy with shame that I were already deceiving her. But truth would come another day. For now, I had a position!

I woke up sudden-like in the middle of the night, with the baby having a bit of a rumble in a strange bed. That was when I heard her words again: *Miss* Mary Finn, she'd said, knowing all along.

JAMES 1888

Morning

Those wooden birds and Mama Peevey were waiting. He stood up and checked his trousers for bits of glass or rubbishy vegetables. What did James have to complain about if Mama was lying there sick? He hobbled on stiff legs back out to the street. He'd go up and down the roads that fanned out from the hospital, he'd walk in the sunny spots, he'd find Mama . . .

He should be at her side, saying, "Jamie is here now. I'll make you a nice cup of tea, shall I?" James imagined taking the kettle down from its hook and filling it with two ladles of water from the barrel by the step. Rainwater's best, Mama Peevey always told him, it's softer than what comes out of the ground. Nicer for tea and nicer for hair. He'd fill the kettle and poke up the fire and hang the kettle on the hob set over the grate . . . and when it began to puff away, he'd take it, careful as anything, holding the handle with that old mitten. . . . James's eyes got a sting thinking of that old gray mitten that used to be Mister's, till Mama knit him new red ones for Christmas just so's she could use the thick gray one for her hot mitt. . . .

Then he'd pour the hissing water into the teapot and give it a swirl to warm the pot, tossing it after out over the back stoop. He'd reach up and take down the tin of tea leaves . . . Oh, that tin! James knew exactly the size and shape in his hands, the TETLEY TEA printed across the side . . . He'd measure out the tea leaves, one for each visitor and one for the pot. He'd pour in water, just a thumb-depth to start, count to sixty while it steeped, then fill the pot.

James could see Mama's fingers crumbling the brown sugar crystals, feel her eyes look at him as she sipped, before smacking her lips to say, "Oh my Jamie, you do make a nice cup, don't you, for such a little fellow?"

Only he wasn't little anymore, was he? He was nearly eleven and he hadn't made a cup of tea in over four years. *But I remember how, Mama. I remember.*

MARY
AUGUST 1878

Labor

Mam's babies used to come at night, or how I recall, anyway. Seems there were always dark in the window. I'd be with the little ones when our dad went with a lantern to fetch Mother Layney, the midwife. She'd come with her bag and sidle into Mam's room, wanting a cup of water to drink from time to time. We'd hear moaning and soothing and keening and finally crying. There the baby'd be.

Well, you'll not want to know the details any more than we did, though it might benefit mothers forever if young men had a brighter ken of how a baby arrives.

I were just tapping the end off Miss Kaye's soft-boiled egg when I were surprised with a flood in my drawers. An upsetting way to start the day. It were then Miss Angela who took up the breakfast tray and notified the old lady that I were no longer on duty. It were then Miss Angela who dithered and worried while I were amazed with the tide sweeping my insides like I were a seaside cove. Lordy, but what a body takes care of without the head having a single say!

Miss Kaye appeared, not in her usual immaculate condition, but in her nightdress with hair awry.

"Have you not gone yet?" she scolded Miss Angela. "And you," she said to me. "Where will we put you?"

We had not given this a moment's thought. Me not having a bed, aside from the mat before the stove, there were no place to curl up as I wanted, nor anywhere to do the birthing. I scuttled about, tidying the kitchen, but then would feel a furious swelling, like a roasted apple so hot it burst its own skin.

A time went by, long or short I do not know. Miss Angela came back with Mrs. Carroll, who had eyed me and rubbed me a few weeks prior with a cluck and a nod. Now she looked at the kitchen table, which were too short for all of me to lie upon, and decided on the chair instead.

"You'll want the arms to push against," she said, and Lordy, she were right. With her nearby, I gave over to the roar and did not try to stop the hollering. Miss Angela did not linger, but dear Miss Kaye were there with chips of ice to slip between my lips and a sponge for my face. She were most curious and fascinated and near drove Mrs. Carroll mad with questions, it being a first for her as well as for me.

And finally, with wrenching, bellowing pain, it were over, lickety-split. Amidst all the wet and blood and twingeing, there you were, as fine a boy as ever came to anyone.

Some people look backward with squinted eyes and bitter hearts, cursing themselves for not seeing happiness while it were staring at them. I were lucky now to have an interlude of utter happiness that I revived in clouded moments forever after.

I knew about babies.

I were big enough when all my brothers got born, and I had our Nan from one day old all to myself. I knew the smallest noise, the wee twitches of the hands, the pee enough for a pony, I knew the smell of the head, the down of the hair, the little soft patch on the skull.

But with all that, I didn't know about having my own. Even Nan, who were cleaved to me, even dear lost Nan were not like having this boy who were the one taught me that a tit can be a gift from Heaven.

Miss Kaye Reed were a dear old lady, and smitten with Johnny as much as a real granny might be. I'd lay him in her lap and she'd marvel, just as if he weren't a fatherless mite who ought to be in the kitchen sleeping in the coal scuttle.

It were one morning, early, when I took up her tea, the way she liked it on a tray in her bed. She never said anything, but why would she hurry down first thing, only to listen to Miss Angela carping, when she could start the morning slowly, like a lady, with a soft-boiled egg and two slices of brown bread with plum jelly?

I settled the tray next to her and drew back the curtains.

"No rain today, Mary?"

"No, ma'am."

"Were you up much in the night? Did Johnny sleep well?"

"Well enough, ma'am. He fussed a bit at five o'clock but that were a help, really, it being time to light the fires."

There were a bit more chatter of that nature before I reached the door, she talking to me often, like a person instead of only a maid, which set Miss Angela's teeth to grinding.

"Can you bring him in to visit when I've finished my breakfast?" she said.

"Yes, Miss Kaye."

I delivered John and even left him with her for a few minutes while I carried her tray to the kitchen before our daily walk. I caught myself humming a tune as I rinsed out her teacup, that were how close to perfect life were behaving that morning.

We took a turn about the square, it being a fresh day. Miss Kaye had a fair stride for a lady of her years, Johnny did some cooing, and I considered how if I began to knit this week, he might possibly have cozy leggings by Christmas.

"You have a fine, fine boy," said Miss Kaye.

"I will not argue with you there." I were not always formal when it were only us.

"His father . . . will be proud, when the time comes for them to meet," she said, careful-like. She waited for me to say, but I only rubbed my nose on Johnny's.

"I haven't held a baby since my niece was born." She had a wee chuckle over that. "That would put it somewhere near sixty years."

She patted him and tugged the blanket up, making him snug as we turned against the wind for the walk back.

"I believe I'll have a rest," said Miss Kaye when we came in. "Oh, goodness, the baby has fallen asleep as well! Aren't we a pair?" She laughed her cheery laugh and off she went to lie down.

Johnny slept while I boiled a chicken, all being peaceful until Miss Angela come to the kitchen with a ghastly look pasted on her face.

"Run to fetch Dr. Dode this minute," she said. "My aunt has died in her sleep."

JAMES 1888

Still Looking

His feet were wet and cold as Coram. He wanted tea himself. And dry clothing, or at least stockings. He'd even welcome gruel.

He tripped and nearly fell. A man caught his arm and pulled him upright, but hurried on without hearing thanks.

James had been dodging people and not paying attention to the houses. What if he'd missed the one with birds? It was too crowded out here, and noisy! He paused for a moment to catch his breath. A woman came along the road, leading a cow at the end of a rope! He'd seen cows before, back in Homefield, in a *meadow,* but here?

"Hey! Don't touch my girl!"

James jumped back before the dairymaid could swat him. He hadn't been touching, really. It smelled too . . . hairy.

All about him the day was starting; merchants called and laid out wares, an ice cart chinked by; a pair of chimney sweeps, still with clean morning faces, were playing swordfight with their brushes.

And there, in front of him, shuffling awkwardly and using both hands to lug a full basket of pies, was the old man, Pie Peter. A familiar face in all the whirl of London!

"Hello," said James. Whiffs of meat and pastry inspired him to speak. "Could I help carry your basket?"

"Clear off," said the pieman. "Gutter thief."

"I'm not a thief, I swear," said James. "Look, I'll pay for a pie." He flipped open his jacket and pointed to the five gleaming buttons he'd kept to the inside. Pie Peter raised furry eyebrows.

"All right, then," he said.

"Have you got a knife?" said James. He mimed cutting off a button.

The trade was made. The first bite of pie left him dizzy with joy. By the time he'd finished, he thought he might be sick, packing in so much so fast. Pie Peter picked at his teeth while he watched James eat. That made James sicker.

"Do you know where there's a house near here that's covered in birds?" said James. "Carved birds?"

Pie Peter spat out a bit of the pick he'd been digging his teeth with. He signaled with his head, off to the left.

"Brunswick Square," he said. "You want another pie?"

Not a chance of that. James hurried away, his feet burning to take him straight to where he was going.

MARY 1878

Telling How It Seemed Like the End

Miss Kaye passing on, sudden like that, were as woeful a thing as ever happened since my own mam's deathbed. Dr. Dode came and agreed that she were dead and gone. I helped Miss Angela wash and dress her, though I'd just done it while she were living a few hours before. How quick a person goes from chattering under the shining sky to being a body with nobody home.

She were laid out on her own bed, tidy and elegant as she always were. Johnny, however, forgot his sunny self and now were in the spirit of mourning. He wailed as if his little soul could not bear to lose Miss Kaye. Miss Angela went about tongue-clicking and head-shaking and shoulder-hunching, most anxious to have him quiet. I tried to nurse and tried to keep him shushed but there were tasks at hand, what with the blinds being lowered, which alerted the neighbors, who began to stop in, and Miss Kaye's room needing to be put straight all around her before visitors could visit. Johnny fussed as if there were a misery contest and he were set on winning. Of all days!

A tall chap came, wearing a tall black hat and a mourning band around his arm, which I suppose were his everyday apparel, him being in the burying trade. The funeral were set for three days on and she'd be lying there with us till then.

While the baby finally napped, I took a cup of tea up to Miss Angela in her room, where she were shifting through a small heap of garments on the quilt.

"I'll be in black for six weeks," she said, "being a niece. I've got the dark bombazine from when Papa passed on, though I'll have to let it out some. . . ." She were only thinking aloud, not asking advice, or I'd have told her those seams weren't wide enough to expand as much as she'd require, with her fondness for buttered bread.

"But I'll need a dress by tomorrow," she said. "Which do you think is more becoming, Mary? The blue or the russet?"

"The blue, miss."

She lingered on the decision but agreed at last. "Take the russet, then. Go to Robinson's Mourning Warehouse in Regent Street. They can dye it black overnight and deliver here tomorrow. And select mourning cards as well. I shall need two dozen with a half-inch border."

"Yes, miss. But Johnny's sleeping, miss."

"Leave him here. And hurry back."

Only when I hustled in an hour later, he were clamoring like a fiend, kicking in his basket, and Miss Angela were cross-eyed with being irked so. It were quite a while longer before he'd settle down to nurse.

Evening came and Miss Angela wanted only broth and toast. Her face were gray with the weight of things and I were right sorry for her until she spoke.

"I must inform you, Mary, that there is no longer a position for you here. My aunt was a charitable woman, but I am not so inclined to provide shelter for . . . for a bastard baby."

My face prickled hot. "I nev—!"

She cut me off with a wave. "Naturally you would object. However, this is now my house. I am mistress here and you will leave tomorrow."

"Tomorrow? But . . . Miss Kaye! The funeral!"

"You'd not be welcome there in any case. I will pay your wages until the end of the month as my aunt would have wanted, bless her giving soul."

The end of the month were four days away so Miss Angela were not being excessive generous.

"Could I not stay until Saturday, miss? There's a terrible lot of preparing . . . and if you're paying me?" My head were swarmed with panic.

"No, Mary, you may not. I have listened to the mewling of your spurious child until I thought I should go mad!"

"But where will I go?" Tomorrow! "How will I find a position? I have . . . Johnny . . ."

"These are questions that you should have considered before you surrendered to immorality. I am really only helping you by sending you on your way. Perhaps now you'll do what you should have done to begin with. Lose the child somewhere. Good night."

She turned herself around, holding the chair against her bum and turning it with her. There were no mistake about the interview—and my good fortune—being at an end.

It were resolve alone that carried me from that hour through the days that followed. There were no more fairy-tale old ladies arriving in carriages. There were no forgive-ness from wicked stepmothers. There were no second chances at marrying the handsome prince or the other one, disguised as a frog. It were early autumn and not dead winter, which is why I am alive to tell the tale.

I began where I'd left off before meeting Miss Kaye, seeking refuge in churches, no matter which saint were on the door. I now were clearly fallen, however, as I had you in my arms, and a woman's folly allows for little kind-ness even from God. Details will not enhance the tale, and remembering won't change the end. All my fears were laid out true before me. You were sickly, I were sicker. One morning I awoke to utter silence, worse by far than hun-gry whimpering. I shook the blanket in alarm and only then did you startle faintly. . . .

My choice were finally this: Go to the workhouse, taking you with me, where death were likely, and, according
to Nut, horrors were certain. Or forsake you, my only precious boy, at the Foundling Hospital, where you might be
raised up not knowing how your mother tried, nor how
she loved you enough to say goodbye.

JAMES 1888

The Byrd House

James worried, would he recognize the Byrd house? And then there it was, birds all over it, just as everyone said, looking ready to burst into song. With Mama being right inside, James was ready to burst into song himself. He could almost hear the organ in the chapel with a swelling "Hallelujah" as he climbed the steps in front.

Knocking on the door would be the only way in. Pray that Mr. Byrd was elsewhere, be ready to start running if he answered. Or it might be a servant, who would care about his grubbiness. James glanced down. No help for it. He could use his smile on a servant.

It was the loony Miss Byrd, though, who replied to the taps of the bird-shaped knocker. A woodpecker, James was pretty certain. Miss Byrd, who'd made all the carvings. She leaned on her cane, head crooked as if asking *why?*

"I like your birds," said James.

"Well, now," she said.

"I'm James. I've come to see my mother."

"They've been searching for you," said Miss Byrd. She looked along the street and back at him, noticing the shabby state of his clothing. "Oh, dear me. Come inside. You'll want a bit of a visit before they find you."

Mama Peevey sat on a chesterfield that was covered in blue flowered fabric, so that she seemed to be resting in a garden. Her feet were tucked up under a blanket but she didn't look poorly otherwise. Her smile was as wide as her arms. James sank into her, kneeling on the floor.

"Mama."

"Oh, my dear lovey. Wherever have you been?"

"They locked me up, Mama. That horrible Mr. Byrd, he put me—"

"Shhh! Jamie!"

Miss Byrd was watching in the doorway, and he'd said a bad thing about her brother. But a true bad thing! She shook her head a little and shrugged.

"He used to lock *me* in the closet when we were children," said Miss Byrd. "Only when I was naughty, of course." She limped to the window and peered into the street. "I'll leave you to have a little visit, but those gents from the hospital will be back, I just know it. Or else the cart will come to take your foster mother home." She crossed the room again. "I'll bring you in some tea."

"Now!" said Mama, taking James's hands. "Tell me everything. You've run away!"

"That's not . . . I haven't actually . . . I only came to see you," said James. He patted her and realized there was a bump in front. She saw him realizing and smiled some more.

"Yes, Jamie, I'm going to have another baby. In just a few weeks, Lord willing. Lizzy won't have to wait long for company. And I'll have another foundling, to go with this one." She pointed to her belly. "Lizzy will be a big sister again. It was terrible hard on her, saying goodbye to Rose."

"So . . . so you're not sick?"

"No, just all done in from the journey, and the upset of you"—she glanced toward the door and finished in a whisper—"of you being dragged off without even a minute together with Rose."

James whispered too. "He's the meanest one. We call him . . . Byrd the Turd."

"Oh, Jamie!" She put her hand over his mouth, but he knew she wasn't angry. She was so familiar, even her hand felt the way it should. He blinked against the sting of tears.

"Is it a terrible place?" Her voice soft, worried.

"The food is disgusting," said James. "But . . . not so bad in other ways. I like the music. I'll be in the choir next year, and if I keep up with my lessons, I'll be in the band. Mr. Chester says—Mr. Chester is the history master and he was a foundling too—he says he played the clarinet, so that's what I'm going to try. He says I have long fingers, and that's the best for clarinet."

Mama looked at him with eyes full of . . . of sugar. "Rose was sad as sad to leave Lizzy, but she knew she'd have you, we told her that."

Worry rustled in James's head. *That's not true,* he nearly said. *I'll hardly see Rose. She's a girl. You shouldn't have made things up.* Life is harder if you have expectations. That was something he knew from coming here. Rose would learn it too. Mama and Mister would never understand.

"What about Mister?" said James. "Does he miss me?"

"Well, he did, of course, in the beginning," said Mama. "But now he's got used to being just with girls. Oh, he sent you something!" She fussed about under the blanket till she'd found her pocket and pulled out a whistle, cut from a stick.

"That's a fine one!" said James. "Tell him thanks." He played a couple of notes, a tiny memory tootling through. "I miss . . . I miss you, Mama. I miss the shop, and Toby, and Mister. I miss Martin. Do you ever see Martin?"

"Oh, he's a wild boy, that Martin!" said Mama. "Last week he stole Lizzy's knickers right off the line and turned them into a flag, of all things!"

Miss Byrd came in, pushing a tea trolley. "If I carry a tray," she said, "we get more tea on the floor than in the cups."

The wheels of the trolley squeaked and wouldn't turn properly. James tried to help but there was a knock on the door and Miss Byrd scuttled out.

James's stomach whooshed. *Not Mr. Byrd, please not!*

"It won't be your Mr. Byrd," said Mama. "He wouldn't knock on his own door, would he?"

"It's the fellow with the cart." Miss Byrd came in. "I've told him to wait right out front. I'll just fetch your shawl and basket."

James helped Mama to unwrap from the blanket.

"I'm nearly as tall as you are, Mama!"

She whispered again. "You could come home with me, Jamie. You've got this far, you could pop right into the cart with me and come home. They'll chase you down eventually, but wouldn't that be a surprise for Lizzy!"

Oh, wouldn't it? He nearly thought so.

"But what about Rose?" And what about Walter? And Mr. Chester? And Full-of-Snot, and the nice new nurse?

"Rose needs you," said Mama. "That's true."

"Do you think . . . when I'm big, Mama, could I come to visit you then?"

"I'd be living with a broken heart if you didn't, Jamie."

"Boy! My brother is coming!" Miss Byrd flung open the door. "Go, now! You can leave through the kitchen, but you must go straight back to the Foundling, you promise me? No shilly-shallying!"

"Yes, miss." James hugged Mama one more time, smelling his childhood. Then he ran.

MARY 1878

⁂

Telling About Leaving Him

The Petition of _Mary Finn_ of _Wayburn_ Humbly Sheweth–

That your petitioner is a _spinster_, _16_ years of age, and was on the _3rd_ day of _August_ delivered of a _male_ child, which is wholly dependent on your petitioner for its support, being deserted by the father. That _Caden Tucker_ is the father of the said child, and was, when your petitioner became acquainted with him, a _groom's boy_, at _barracks of Coventry guard_,

London, and your petitioner last saw him on the _12th_ day of _January_, and believes he is now _posted to Afghanistan with no intention of responsibility_. Your petitioner therefore humbly prays that you will be pleased to receive the said child into the aforesaid hospital.

The gentleman at the desk wore ribbed white stockings that I noticed because I were looking groundward, not into his face. How did he keep white stockings so white, I wondered. All that mud out there and not even a splash on him! Perhaps he saved a clean pair in a basket under his desk and removed the soiled ones when he arrived each day? Or perhaps he didn't _arrive,_ perhaps he _lived_ there and never exposed his legs to the mucky streets of London, the narrow sloshing gutters on Lamb's Conduit Street.

"Miss Finn?"

"Uh, yes, sir?" I were that distracted that I wondered if I'd mentioned his hose aloud. My arms were squeezing Johnny so tight he woke and struggled.

"Shh," I whispered, and quick glanced at the waiting man. A woman stood quietly behind him, wearing a uniform of sorts, with a broad white apron, also very clean.

"I have your letter here," he said, tapping a paper that I supposed to be mine.

"And I wrote it myself, sir. I've learned my letters, and it took some time, but I put all the words down there myself."

"Good for you."

What did I go telling him that for? It made me sound stupid, not clever.

"Nurse Aldercott will take the child now. You may have a minute to say goodbye, but no longer. There are others waiting. He'll be baptized here in the chapel and taken off to a country foster home in the morning, where he will be nursed and cared for until he is ready to return here for his education. You may rest assured that he is in the best of hands."

He tipped his head at me, like a bow were intended but I were too inconsiderable for him to take the trouble to bend at the waist.

"Good day," he said, and went away through the door. The woman with the apron stepped forward and I stepped backward.

"Just a little moment, ma'am." I were croaky already and turned away quick. I stood by the draperies at the window, holding my cheek to Johnny's cheek.

"All the things you'll know," I whispered. "All what I don't know. You'll be eating, and with sturdy clothes on you. You'll have lessons, and be reading before you're grown. You'll meet dozens of boys . . . friends . . . maybe they'll feel like brothers. . . ." A picture of Thomas and Davy blinked in my mind and a terrible flash of Small John when I last saw him, with his cap on backward and his teeth knocked out from falling off the fence.

"You'll knock somebody's teeth out one day," I told my boy. "He'll call you a . . . a motherless brat, and you'll squint those blue eyes and say 'What did you call me?' And you'll push up your sleeves and give him a sock in the eye, won't you, Johnny? You tell him you've got a mother and she loves you . . . she loves you . . . I love you. . . ."

I tucked Caden's silver button between the folds of the blanket. I kissed him. And that were goodbye.

The matron took him, turning his face to her shoulder, pulling the blanket up to cover his head so I couldn't see him anymore.

"I wonder, ma'am, could I ask you, please? I'm a very good worker, harder than anything. I've been in service over two years now. I helped at an inn, with all that cooking, and linens changed every day in all those rooms. I worked in a big house, too, so I can haul up and down stairs with no complaints, I've done my share of laundry—"

She put a hand on my arm, firm but not harsh, and shook her head.

"No, dear. The mothers are not permitted to work here, we're to shoo you off at once."

"Oh, but it's not to do with my . . . my boy . . ." The word caught in my throat as if I'd swallowed a plum and it sat, whole, wrapped around that word *boy*, and I knew I'd never breathe right again. "I need work."

"You'll forget this trouble in a year or two," she said. "We all forget who's come and who's gone."

She took me gently to the door and that were that.

Wandering down that Foundling Hospital drive, I were unsteady of foot and foggy of mind. Putting a boot down, moving the other one to join it, putting a boot down again—it seemed beyond me. Finally I were outside the gates and stood a-swaying till a gent in a black coat came out of the little guardhouse and said to "move along, miss, there'll be no loitering here."

How many girls had already been on this spot, loitering? All those children behind the big gate, they'd all got mothers somewhere, hadn't they? And every one of those mothers likely felt as I did, numb and spooked and sorrowful. And there were no one to tell, no person I could look in the face to say, *I've delivered my baby to strangers. To save his life or mine?*

I pressed my hand against the wall, needing that wall for a moment, wondering if they'd built it for this very purpose to hold the mothers up. I made my way, one wee step after another, one hand always pushing against the gritty stones. Some time later, though it were no distance really, I got myself to St. George's cemetery, tucked behind the hospital grounds.

I wished it were St. Bartholomew's churchyard, with Mam nearby, but then I thought of Margaret Huckle's children, frolicking about on a Sunday. That made me laugh to myself, though I were prickle-eyed already. It were laughing that recalled me, an itch that life weren't over, even as I were headed to a burial place with the dreadest of intents.

Once I landed there, I ambled around for a bit, walking steadier now, being in the right place for my intentions. I were looking for the little stones, knowing they always keep a corner special for babies and children taken before their time. Sure enough, there it were, under a weeping willow, wouldn't you know, most of the markers no higher than my knee.

I took my time, reading slow and careful as Eliza showed me, so I understood every word, devoted to choosing the very one.

Sophia Giller
Little Angel
July 14, 1859–August 12, 1859

There were a real little angel carved into the top of the marble, but I wanted a boy.

Roddy Bowman
Oct 1862–April 1863
Lies with God

I weren't trusting God as a guardian right then, hoping the place I'd found would be more practical.

And then I saw it, a gray stone about the size of a coal bucket, poking its way through brambles and with a wild rose even, though not tended in a long while.

Felix Kenner
Our son
1822-1824
Not dead but only sleeping

That seemed right. Not dead, I liked that. I knelt most fervently, and with my hands clipped the too-grown, too-green grass away from the face of the gravestone, tears finally burning across my cheeks. I could come to Felix Kenner whenever I wanted a quiet spot. That matron saying *We all forget who's come and who's gone* . . . Not likely!

I hesitate to tell how much I carried on, cloaked in mournfulness so heavy I were kneeling there the longest time. I suppose it's the same for all of us in sorrowful hours, has been always, and forever will be, especially a parent saying goodbye to a child, the worst hour of any. Even knowing that better is to come.

The cold finally seeped through to my bones. My knees were drenched in icy mud so standing up were miserable. Lordy, and nowhere to sleep.

Hard to imagine that without you there might now be a place somewhere for me.

OLIVER 1888

When James Came In

Oliver's relief was an embarrassing rash, best kept hidden. If anyone suspected that this dear, odd little boy mattered to him more than the others . . . There were too many children to let oneself care for a single one, that was how the masters were instructed, and that was what he knew from having been amongst them. No one should care overmuch for a nobody. That was what they said.

Seeing James unharmed, and even cheeky . . . Oliver couldn't speak, his mouth being so dry, and likely better that way. Nothing would slip out that he'd feel foolish about later. He squeezed the boy's pale, dirty wrist and whispered, "Good chap." That new nurse was hovering closer than he'd like. Oliver blinked in the dark hallway, hands clamped inside his pockets to stop from looking as though there was anything to wipe away behind the blink.

A surprise the next minute; the nurse herself was crying, or pretending not to. She'd better toughen up if she hoped to work here for any length of time. You couldn't go around shedding tears over boys you knew nothing about.

"Welcome home, James!" Her voice was cheery despite the wobble, so she knew what was expected even if she couldn't pull it off just yet.

"Hello," said James.

"You've stirred up a fury of worry," said Oliver. "You'll be doing extra chores for weeks."

"Do you suppose I'll be flogged?" said James.

"Flogged? Do you think you live in Roman times?" Oliver thanked the boy silently for banishing the anguish from his heart. "Just a light whipping," he said.

"He'll be *whipped*?" said the nurse.

Oliver winked at James, who solemnly winked back.

"That's all right," said James. "I'm used to it. Usually only forty lashes."

"Ah," said the nurse, catching on. "And I've heard they sprinkle the wounds with salt and lemon juice between strokes."

"I see you know boys," said Oliver. "We met another time, a while ago. I'm Mr. Chester. Oliver Chester." He put out his hand.

"Yes," she said, taking it. "I'm Nurse Finn."

Her hand trembled slightly, as light as a leaf, for the moment Oliver held it.

"You do pong something awful," Oliver said to James. "Did you sleep on a rubbish heap?"

"I think so." James grinned, so pleased with himself. "I am sorry if I caused any trouble. But I did terribly want to see my mama."

"Of course you did," said the nurse. "And she wanted to see you too. You'll both feel better now, going onward."

MARY 1893

Not Telling

I'd be richer than Lady Allyn if I'd got sixpence every time I imagined telling you your own beginnings. Your eyes'd light up, you'd toss your arms about me like a favorite puppy, and we'd have a right old reunion.

Still, there were as many times when my heart turned over with a sickly thump, picturing the other likelihood— that your face'd go gray and you'd spit out regret that'd rip through me like a knife across a rabbit's belly. What tied my tongue for certain were remembering how Johnny . . . how Mrs. Peevey loves her James, and he loves her.

You only need to have a mother, not that it be me.

So, it were better I kept mum, then *and* now. I've seen you grow up a little, all the way to fifteen; fine and handsome just like your daddy, though I confess his features have smudged in my memory, something that were not expected to happen.

Today will never be the end of things, despite saying goodbye. I'll watch from the chapel gallery when you shake hands with the governors and take your certificate. My whole self will swell up, proud as . . . as a mother, and you'll go off wearing new clothes. A manly coat, not a uniform.

Your Mr. Chester says it's usually girls who are clever enough to take a place at the university, but here you are! Going off with shoulders squared and who knows how many footsteps in those new boots? Won't your Peevey family be tickled to bits, when you have your holiday week with them?

I say "your Mr. Chester," but I believe that he is, perhaps, becoming mine too. This leads to that. So you've not said farewell to either of us. No ending here, only another beginning. Do your best, my boy. Be brave and be merry.

Afterword

The characters in this book come entirely from my imagination. But Thomas Coram and his Foundling Hospital were very real, and responsible for saving thousands of lives during more than two hundred years. The good work is continued today by an organization called the Coram Family, which assists inner-city children in London.

Thomas Coram's own mother died when he was four years old. It seems likely that he first sailed to sea by the time he was eleven. He grew up to be a sea merchant and spent many years in America, trading in lumber. Upon his return to England later in life, he was horrified to discover that dead or dying babies were often abandoned in the gutters or dung heaps of London by parents unable to care for them. The only alternative for the very poor was the workhouse, a grim place where families were separated, underfed, and worked like slaves.

Thomas Coram vowed to provide a home that would welcome and educate children born out of wedlock, raising them to be responsible citizens. His dogged efforts for seventeen years resulted finally, in 1739, in King George II's signing a charter to establish the Foundling Hospital.

It was immediately clear, when the doors were opened, that there were far more infants in need than there were places for them. Desperate women crowded the streets, begging that their babies be taken in. Police were hired to patrol the neighborhood so that discouraged mothers would not simply drop rejected babies in the gutter.

Several plans for reception were tried over the next few decades, from undiscriminating universal acceptance to strict guidelines as to the age and health of the child. My character, Mary Finn—and my great-grandmother, Elizabeth Ann Ranson—came to the Foundling Hospital in the late 1800s, when the women were personally interviewed and required to declare that their pregnancy was their first—and last—misstep. The facts of these interviews were carefully recorded and checked. An effort was made to contact each father, to prove that he could not, or would not, provide for his family. Elizabeth Ann, like Mary, was lucky to find a generous employer who allowed the baby to be born under her roof. We'll never know the reason why she made the heartbreaking decision, when her son was nine months old, to say goodbye.

Upon arrival at the hospital, the foundlings were bap-tized with new names, bestowed with a set of clothes, and sent at once to foster mothers in the country, who usually had their own new babies and plenty of milk to nurse an extra. At the age of five or six, the children were returned to the institution to be educated and trained for future use to society—the boys most often as soldiers or sailors and the girls as domestic servants.

I knew none of this when simple curiosity compelled me to learn more about my grandfather's origins—beyond the "orphan" label he'd carried in family lore. He was far from an orphan. Both his parents had been very much alive. He had more of a history than he ever knew—but isn't that true for all of us?

marthe jocelyn

is the author of several award-winning novels and has also written and illustrated picture books. Her novels for Wendy Lamb Books include *How It Happened in Peach Hill* and *Would You*. She lives in Stratford, Ontario.